It Wasn't Always Late Summer

By Ray Noble

To my family and with particular thanks to Elle, Penny, Denis and Tiffy.

Chapter One: Annie

It wasn't always a sunny afternoon in late summer, but so it seemed to Annie basking in the sun, loving the warmth she could only imagine, remembering the band playing sweetly on the now deserted and ruined stand, beating time with the big bass drum. She had watched the bandstand fade where once she sat with her mother listening to the brass band from the factory, the old factory belching smoke, a soft stream of white rising silently skywards from its tall chimney. The factory was where her father had worked long hours in his dark blue, stained overalls smelling of grease and engine-oil. Silently casting a long shadow on the landscape, the rumble of the factory ceased with the final sound of the siren at the end of the working day. Once, it was there, the sound. Now it had gone. She listened hopefully, but it had not returned. There was only a ghostly presence where once they trod, the tramping boots of the workers and the ringing of bicycle bells. Now birds sang where once there had been the constant rumbling of engines, wheels turning, pistons pumping, the loud hiss of steam, the rattling and jangling of thick metal chains – chains, rusted red-brown, still clinging to the pulleys on which they were hung, silent now but for the occasional windswept creaking.

And in the park, the once bright red, white and green painted façade of the Victorian bandstand had faded with time and from the rain, had been scratched away with a diligent pen-knife, and was emblazoned with inane graffiti, a declaration of love, or that 'kilroy woz ere'. Here were the messages echoing in time; here, where the band had played when the pals from the factory had gone to be slaughtered on the Somme, her granddad had said. Here they had played for those who returned, and for those who had not. Here they had played again for the lost souls and those killed in the Blitz and the soldiers who didn't return. Here they had played when the factory closed. Here they had marked time until their time too had come. Here was Annie's death.

Unseen on the solid wooden bench by the lake, Annie enjoyed the ducks with their continuous chatter, preening their shiny, iridescent feathers in the sun, splashing the water, heads bobbing, ducking and diving with tails in the air. Swans glided gracefully, heads held high. Annie remembered the Trumpet Voluntary echoing now distantly through time. A gentle breeze rippled the water, and a model yacht with tattered sails snagged on a tangled knot of a fallen tree and boys had thrown stones in a forlorn attempt to set it free. A trumpet solo, crisp and clear, brightly pierced the dull heat of the day, played by a young man in a neatly-pressed tunic who had gone for an audition for a scholarship to study at the Royal College of Music, they said. Annie's mother had felt as proud as if he had been one of her own. "Oh, Annie, how wonderful!" she had exclaimed, gently squeezing Annie's hand. "Isn't that splendid?" And so it was, Annie thought. Annie remembered it was 1953 because it was the year of the Queen's coronation and she had been given a spoon with a crown on its handle.

Annie remembered the fun fair, with its painted wild horses galloping faster and faster, balloons, pink candy floss and music in the night, and the smell of hot dogs and onions. How different it was in the daytime with children, lots of them, shouting and screaming, running, skipping and hopping, and eating ice-cream and lollipops. In the night there were teenagers, shouting and screaming, running, and eating ice-cream and lollipops. Annie saw it all: the games they played, the hide and seek, the giggles, the cuddles, the stolen kisses, and more, much more. In the night, the wind created phantoms rustling the bushes and trees, and there were monstrous moon-cast shapes and the rustlings of animals scampering through the grass. Annie was the cold wind of the night, the shiver of a moment, the eternal cry of a lost soul. Unaware of her, seeing her balloon, a boy or girl would reach out to catch it, but it would pull away, floating skyward into a tree. They sensed a presence unexplained – a feeling, a wisp of wind, a touch – but they couldn't see Annie. A lad would climb into the tree to fetch the balloon as it escaped, floating higher through the branches. A girl urged him to climb higher: "He's almost got it! Fetch it, Barry! Climb higher!" Balancing tenuously on a branch, stretching his body, he would reach up, now on tip-toe a few more inches at a stretch, while Annie feared he would fall. They would never catch it, of course, but wondering what would happen if they did, to break the spell, to catch the time and set her free, Annie sometimes hoped they would.

Sometimes bright red, sometimes a faded pink, more often the balloon wasn't there at all. Sometimes it was a deflated reminder of past joys swept up with the leaves. The children got the closest, and sometimes it would allow a child to touch it, but only just, and only by the very tips of their fingers. "I touched it! I touched it!" they would cry, their mums pulling them away and telling them not to be so silly. It was the children who sensed how special it was, how different it was. Walking with their mothers, they still came to the fair just as she had done – but now the childhood friends she had played with were mothers themselves, like Rose, who had been her best friend, and who now had a daughter, Mary. She watched them grow, as she would not. These were the children she'd known and who had played noisily in clusters in the street, on the swings and roundabouts, or sitting in school doing their times-tables. She'd liked twelve times twelve the most; there was something about twelve that she liked, but she never knew why. A 'dozen' and then there were 'dozens and dozens', which was a lot, and a baker's dozen, which was very peculiar. She'd also liked yellow and green in preference to blue and red, and she thought the Union Jack would be much better if it was yellow, white and green, not red, white and blue. She'd painted snowflakes and Father Christmas, holly and berries on the school-room windows. They'd run in the cold, crisp snow in Wellington boots and flowing hand-knitted scarves. They'd write words with a pencil in their little red or green spelling books and struggle with their confusion of double l's or r's and 'its' and 'it's'. She saw them now as she might have been: a mother with a child.

And then, when the teenagers came, there would often be music from a portable radio, and she would dance merrily, silently, with the wind blowing the leaves into swirls, with her balloon bobbing, ducking and diving while its string wiggled in a balloon dance. One song in particular she had liked the most. It was on old song by someone called Chuck Berry about 'riding along in my automobile' and 'with no particular place to go'. She'd dance and prance to Chuck Berry, floating in the air, higher and higher, until she could see the distant church steeple poking above the trees in the light of the moon, diminished now by the drab, grey concrete tower blocks where many of the children lived.

She witnessed the yellow bulldozers, the cranes and the heavy, swinging demolition balls knocking down the rows of terraced back-to-back houses, a whole house taken in one sweep, as though it had been made from cardboard; thin and insubstantial. Gone was the cosy protection, the warmth they had provided, the love, hopes and fears they contained, and the secrets they kept – a death, a birth, mothers, fathers, grandparents who came before, long ago. Peeling floral wallpapered walls in dark greens and reds, painted banisters, creamy white and brown with carpets worn where once children ran up to bed. Sunday lunch: roast potatoes and peas, salad for tea, jam and marmalade at breakfast.

Annie's street, her house, had been amongst the demolished buildings – the house where she was born, and where she had lived for nine happy years. The house where her father came home from the night shift and where she had heard the sound of milk bottles and the gentle hum of the milk float, stopping and starting as it made its way up the hill. The smell of bacon sizzling in the pan with tomatoes and eggs, fried bread and beans, and the whistle she could hear when the kettle boiled for the mugs of tea, cups and saucers on Sundays, with the milk the milkman had left. The smell of gas from the stove, the warmth of a coal fire, the smell of coal and soot, the sound of the coal scuttle, the baker's van and the baker's driver with his leather money bag strapped to his waist, who would leave bread and give her a chocolate cupcake with heaps of dark, sweet chocolate.

Tall tower blocks of concrete reaching for the clouds in the sky, the new estate was a sign of things moving on, of people moving out and people moving in; new people with different lives and stories to tell, and different colours and smells. Sentinel giants towering over the landscape, spying all around, allowing no place to hide – an intrusive laying bare where once were secrets lurking in the dark. No longer was there the smoke from the chimneys or the glowing hearths giving warmth to the families within, but little boxes piled up high.

Once, sitting silently next to her on the bench, her mother would talk to her, whispering softly. Annie wondered if her mother could sense her presence; often her mother cried, wiping away the tears with a light blue tissue smelling of lavender. Once a year, she would bring flowers and leave them for Annie, arranging them in a small vase that she placed at the foot of a tree. Yellow daffodils were her favourite. "Happy birthday, Annie love!" she would say softly with a trembling voice, holding back the tears. "Happy birthday sweetheart!"

Annie's father came too, when he could. His loss, Annie knew, was no less, and his love undiminished, wrapping her in warmth. They sat in silence on the bench. "It's time to let go, lass!" he had said gently, in his soft rumbling voice, warm and rich and full of Christmas, Annie thought, with silver tinsel, and full of the coal dust and the years of work in the factory. He reminded Annie of the coal fire burning in the grate, flames dancing and licking the red-hot embers, the sparks leaping when he poked it and brought it back to life, and of a Christmas tree in the corner with its fairy lights and bells. Her father was all these and more. She wished now that she could roll up in front of the fire, secure in the warm comfort of home, and fall asleep as once she had, and awake to a pillowcase full of fruit, an apple, an orange, perhaps a pear, and a toy.

Annie had been surprised when her father had seen her balloon. He pointed it out to her mother, putting his hand on her shoulder as they walked toward the bench. He stopped for a moment, squinting into the sun, but when he looked again it had gone, or it hadn't been there at all. This is what it was like with Annie: she would catch the imagination, an ephemeral presence, and then be gone. A falling leaf caught by the wind; a reflection in the water; a brief momentary apparition; a feeling; a wish; a hope; a beat of the heart.

Pulling desperately on the string, trying hard to make the balloon appear, Annie wished her father to see it again. But he didn't, and then she wondered if he had seen it at all. It was a wishful thought, a hope, a beat of the heart; just a few leaves, gold and red, swirling in the wind.

Her mum's head resting on his big chest, her father had whispered again, softly, "It's time to let go, love!"

Her mother had returned to the bench once or twice. She sat and talked, and this was how Annie knew of some of the things that had happened to Uncle Tom and his dog. But there were things that Annie knew, that Annie could see, of which she knew her mother would be unaware – like how sometimes she saw Uncle Tom's dog running, jumping, wagging his tail, panting with his long tongue flopping with his equally long ears as he bounded across the park towards her. Uncle Tom's dog had barked at Annie's balloon and Uncle Tom had a puzzled expression as he pulled the dog away. "Hello, Uncle Tom! It's me, Annie!" she had cried with joy. But he hadn't heard, of course, and Shep the dog had sneezed, taken one more glance at her balloon, and trotted off at his feet. Now Uncle Tom's dog was long gone, and Uncle Tom was gone too.

"He passed away peacefully, Annie love, in his sleep," her mum had said. "And it was a mercy, love, because he had suffered so much those last few months. But perhaps you already know that, dear. Perhaps he's with you now!"

But no: nobody was with Annie, because Annie was lost.

It took time for Annie to accept her death. She couldn't sense much at first. It took time before she became aware of people and objects. It wasn't a sense as such – it was just a 'was', a being, or a 'not'. She had expected someone to come and collect her, but nobody did. So there she was – or wasn't, as Annie had mused later. She had been the kind of girl that readily got lost, so she had simply assumed that this is what she was: lost and confused. Her mother also had assumed that she was lost. Perhaps she had wandered off and was lost. She wouldn't be far. She was never far away, was Annie. "She could get lost at the end of our garden, could Annie!" But she wasn't lost, not this time. Her mother had looked for her, and her father had looked for her in the dim light of dawn when he got home from the night shift. But by then Annie's mother had called the police from the call box at the bottom of the hill, and for several days a line of policemen with helmets and others with sticks picked their way methodically over the park, poking in shrubs, probing the soil, and searching in the woods . Annie wasn't lost; she was missing, and as each day passed, as each week, and month and year passed, it was clear that she was gone. And the fretful searching turned to an agonising wait, a dull pain, a persistent hunger, an irremediable loss.

Chapter Two: Mary

Pulling back the curtain just a little, so as not to wake her partner Paul, a shard of light from the clear blue sky lit Mary's pale face, casting her shadow on the bedroom wall. The clear view across the park from the tenth-floor flat was stunning, the lake glistening blue-green – the colour of Mary's eyes – and beyond it the dense cluster of trees, their canopy like painted dark green wads of cotton wool. Beyond that was an expanse of grass where the children played cricket or soccer, or ran around incomprehensibly on invisible horses. There was a copse here, another there, and a wood beyond where they played Robin Hood and ran for Coke and ice cream at the wooden café by the old bandstand where Mary had once served tea and iced buns and buttered bacon sandwiches in the school holidays.

Compensating little for the creaky lifts, which were more often than not out of action, the expansive vista was the only bright aspect of the concrete-and-glass blocks of flats. The lifts stank like toilets, and the walls were covered with graffiti: egregious words or pictures carved with knives or other sharp implements, and gross pictures leaving little to the imagination, carved by people with limited artistic flair. The strange, aerosol-sprayed, bright coloured or black signs were like primeval symbols from a lost tribe – one gang's blazing statement of hegemony over another, territorial markings like cats pissing on a shrub. Mary thought it was as if the people were crapping on themselves, because few people other than the tenants saw these statements or the occasional official from the council. They were an eternal scream within the bowels of the building; 'get me out of here!', or, simply, 'fuck you!' Mary believed it was the result of utter boredom and couldn't-care-less attitude, the head-banging of a broken, dysfunctional community.

"People don't care no more," her mum would say, "not like when I was a kiddie, they don't."

"Yes, right, Mum."

"They do as they please; no discipline or respect."

"Yes, Mum."

"Not like it was when we grew up. Our parents wouldn't have allowed it, I can tell you that."

"Right, Mum."

And her mum was probably right, Mary thought: it wasn't like it was in the old days. But this is where they were: on the tenth floor of a grey tower block.

Carried now to the world beyond the rolling hills, Mary followed the railway, across the bridge, with trains a distant clatter on the track, carrying people to and from the sprawling suburbs of the once distinct town with its churches and steeples, congregations and Baptist ministries, itself now a greater suburb of the city beyond. She remembered that the train, looking like a toy in the distance, had carried her with Mum and Dad to the seaside on a day trip – a journey more fun than the day itself on the shingle beach where the wind blew too hard and carried the deckchair away together with her mum's hat. They had fish and chips from a shop on the corner, with masses of salt and vinegar, watching the gulls diving for fish and the small sailing boats out at sea, tacking first this way and then that. Her dad had carried her on his shoulders, feet crunching on the shingles, singing that silly song "Oh, I do like to be beside the seaside. Oh, I do like to be beside the sea!" But he couldn't remember all the words, and they had laughed as he had *rumpty-timpty-tummed* it. And then on the journey back, she'd fallen asleep, and awoke next morning in her bed as though it had been an exciting dream. How free it was, the land beyond the hills, she thought: free of care, a moment of peace, a moment of joy, and how it might have been in a childhood dream.

Mary looked down now on the streets of the estate. With just small flecks of cloud in a windless sky, the mid-morning sun beat down on the corrugated-iron boarded-up windows of the short parade of shops, too hot for the black cat searching desperately for shade. The parade was infested at night by junkies and prostitutes and rats, and known locally as *Needle Alley*. Mary wondered what shops they had been; a butcher's or a baker's shop? No doubt a newsagent and tobacconist too – a newsagents' and sweetshop run by a family from Bangladesh who had long since made their escape from the stones and insults.

There had been a little toy shop, her mum had said, run by a Mrs Robinson. "She was a lovely lady, was Mrs Robinson! We used to go to her shop when you were little, Mary. Don't you remember?"

"Oh yes, I remember," she had replied. But Mary couldn't remember, not really. She had only the haziest recollection of a time before – a lost time, as though she had been reborn with disconnected memories of a past life. Faces and places disappeared when she tried to recall them. Her mum often confused time. Her mum was always talking about the time before – of the 'old days', 'the good days', the 'not-like-it-is-now' days. Much of it was before Mary was born. She was sure the toy shop was before she was born, although she did remember a puppet with strings – a girl, it was – that she could make walk up and down and bow or courtesy. She made it sing and dance for her dad, who laughed and patted her head.

"Well, of course you were just a nipper then!" her mum reassured her, sensing that she couldn't really remember. Her mum was always talking about when Mary was 'a nipper', as if there was something very important she had to remember. Mary wished she could be 'a nipper' again. It wasn't that long ago when she was 'a nipper', but it seemed an age, a time before.

"When this estate first opened and people moved in, they was local," her mum said. "And the shops was where we used to meet up. There was a post office, a greengrocer's. They'd all been there before the estate, see? When there was houses what people lived in."

"Yes, Mum."

"We lived in them houses when we was growing up, Mary." Rose nodded in the direction of the estate, where the houses used to be.

"Yes, Mum."

"Things was different then, Mary love."

"Right, Mum."

Yes, things were different, and Mary sighed for the lost innocence. Even the estate had been different; now it was a lost world. Before the tower blocks had been built there had been the maisonettes, rows of them neatly lined up with little gardens front and back. They had been the vanguard of the new wave after demolition of the old Victorian houses. Neat and pretty though the Maisonettes had once been, they were now shabby and worn with peeling paintwork where once there had been well-kept blue doors and white trims. Even when they built the tower blocks, they had been well kept. Families moved in, displaced by the clearance of the 'slums' they had lived in previously.

With a caretaker looking after the grounds, there had been fruit trees that he pruned each year – apples mostly, and a pear, her mum had said – and when the fruit was ripe he shared it out. The launderette was there, where mothers met and sullen-faced men sat in front of the dryers, reading the sports pages of crumpled newspapers, discussing the runners and riders and effortlessly grunting this and that at the perpetual chatter of the women. Time was marked by the Grand National, the Boat Race, and the Derby, all passing as flakes of time – a time for a pint to celebrate and a time for bingo in the old cinema where they had once watched *The Dam Busters*, and where there had been Saturday morning pictures with *The Lone Ranger* or *Robin Hood*.

"They never took care of them, Mary."

"Who didn't? Care of what, Mum?"

"The estates. They never took care of them! Wasn't long before they cut this and cut that. And then people had to move away, see, on account of there being no work once they closed the factory."

"There's no work even now, Mum. Least not round here," Mary reflected realistically.

"It's not like it was in the old days."

"No, Mum, not like the old days."

But Mary didn't know the 'old days'; it was like a fairy tale – a place that was, a never-land or a might have been. A silent movie flashing on a screen; people, faces, places in a bygone time.

Now the shops were gone, along with the caretakers and the fruit trees, and they had to catch a bus to the other side of town to the large supermarket and shopping mall. The long trudge there and back with Michelle in the push chair was exhausting. The only cars on the estate were wheel-less junks of scrap supported on bricks, red and rusting and long since abandoned from a hapless joyride, or simply burnt out, wrecked, uninsured, untaxed, junked, dumped – another piece of crap, the burnt-out embers of time, an unintended movie backdrop

Her daughter Michelle, now two years old, was the only reason Mary was here. The council had housed her in the flat because she was a single mother with a baby. Mary herself was eighteen, approaching nineteen. Sometimes she felt glad and happy, especially when the sun was shining, but often she felt sad. When Michelle cried it was difficult, trapped in the small flat with no money or freedom. Mary would cry too, sometimes, with the damp stink of wet nappies, but at least that was over. Now it was a wet bed, which they said she would soon grow out of. Nobody knew, she thought, how much a baby pees. She wanted to escape – not from her child, who she loved, but to a new life for them both. To open the window and fly. Sometimes she felt she could, just as she dreamed she could when she was little, flying past the library window, watching the readers with their newspapers and books. It was all so real that sometimes she didn't know whether she really could fly or not. Now she was too heavy, for sure, but when she was younger, when she was lighter than air, she could fly – in that time when dreams and reality drifted seamlessly day by day, for then the puppet could dance without her strings. How simple it would be, to fly like the pink balloon she saw hovering over the trees in the park. Paul could never see it, even when she pointed it out. She assumed he just couldn't see far enough into the distance, and of course there were many balloons, remnants of a nightly reverie perhaps, snagged on a tree.

"Oh, yes! It's just your imagining, Mary, as usual." Paul had said sceptically.

"Well, I did see it! So there!" Mary had replied dejectedly.

"In any case, it's only a fucking balloon. Jesus, Mary, you don't half go on, girl!"

Paul was not the most articulate person, grunting where words might be uttered. Never particularly observant, he appeared, Mary thought, rarely to see the beauty of the trees and the flowers – or if he did, he never remarked on it – and he never smelled the scent of a flower even when she pushed it under his nose. He would pull away as if it smelled foul, or he simply grunted and took it as another opportunity to grope her breasts.

"This is the best flower," he would say.

"Paul! Don't do that!"

She would grab his hands and pull them away. Any unexpected touch created a tension, an uncontrollable urge to scream, an inward echo in her soul.

"Why not?"

"It's not nice."

"Well, you liked it enough last night!"

"That's not the same."

"The same to me, love."

"Well, it's not nice, and I don't like it."

It wasn't the same the gentle touch, the warmth of the bodies entwined. It wasn't the same, and, really, Paul knew it wasn't the same.

Sometimes Mary thought he was only interested in sex, and sometimes – it depended on the drink – he grunted through that before rolling over and falling asleep. And even then he grunted: grunt, grunt, grunt. Sometimes she wished he wasn't there. But she would be lonely, and loneliness was a darker hole. She didn't want to be alone. Feeling guilty of such thoughts, she would love him even more. As she did now as he lay sleeping.

Paul was not Michelle's father, but he had taken at least some responsibility since moving in with them. That wasn't to say he took much interest – he didn't, or at least not when changing dirty nappies came into it. That was not something he would do, or even contemplate doing. But, given half a chance, Michelle thought, he would make a good dad. Children disarmed him, relaxed him, soothed him, and uncoiled the tight spring. There was gentleness about him when it came to children, and he was considerate and caring about Mary as a mother. And little Michelle really liked Paul. She was always placing her grubby, chocolate-coated fingers on his knee or on his face, whichever was within reach. He was twenty-three, going on seventeen. It wasn't that he was dumb; he was street-wise. He could handle himself and that was useful for Mary in the seedy, dark dangers of the estate. To mess with her was to mess with him, and he had street credibility. Everyone knew that. He wasn't to be messed with.

"You can't show 'em no weakness, girl, see," he would say. "So you make them know they'd best not fucking go there." He'd impressed this on Mary often enough.

He was like a tightly wound spring, Mary thought, waiting to be sprung – tense, explosive, with fists as hard as iron and a tattooed neck saying "fuck with me and you're dead". He'd head-butt first just on a look – better safe than sorry, and attack the best form of defence. And so often she had seen it; a fight down the pub. And when people passed them in the street, they would nod to Paul. "All right, Paul?" Or sometimes they would cross the road or turn away shiftily. Sometimes Mary saw also a warmth behind his cold blue eyes of steel – a glimpse, a shard of light into his inner soul. She saw the lost, needy child within.

"Jesus, Mary, she's put fucking chocolate all over my jeans! You'll have to wash them now! And my fucking shirt!"

Sometimes, not always!

And behind the solid steel door, he was like a boiled sweet with a soft centre, Mary mused: soft and fruity and deliciously caring. Like he had been when they first met. And when he opened up about his father, it all made sense. Mary had lost her dad through death; Paul never found the relationship he wanted with his. His father had been a brute beating up on his own kid. "You can't show 'em no weakness." It all made some kind of sense, his survival mode. But what she hated most was his mood swings. Sometimes he was deeply depressed: morbid and dark, like he was in a deep cavern with no way out. Then he could be impossible, and then she could hate him – hate him because she couldn't reach him, and couldn't know him. He became a stranger, someone she couldn't touch and couldn't feel empathy for. He was somewhere else and not with her; she was pushed away into a cold place where reason played no part.

Paul's preoccupation with sex seemed to colour his view of the world, which was always "fucking something or other": "fucking this or fucking that"; all geezers were "fucking geezers"; everything good was "fucking good"; a bus was a "fucking bus" that you had to wait for at a "fucking bus stop". When the bus came, it was "always fucking late", and when it appeared it was always greeted with "at fucking last!", the bus driver was a "fucking Paki!" and the seats were "fucking shit".

Mary always felt that Paul was about to head-butt someone. He seemed suspicious of everyone. Everyone was out to "fucking do you", and Mary thought that he was probably "fucking right too!"

"Fucking never trust no fucking one, girl!" he would say, matter-of-fact.

This was the most profound statement he had ever made. "Fucking" was Paul's comfort blanket, and without it he would be lost. He didn't seem to understand anything without it. If Mary suggested something was good, he would look puzzled. Good just didn't exist, only shades of bad – fucking bad. If she said something was "fucking good", he would say, "Yeah, like fucking shit!", punching the air with his fist and curling his lip in a sneaky grin, which Mary thought hid a deeper shyness – a self-consciousness that meant he didn't like to be looked at. He didn't want to be known, because to be known was a weakness and vulnerability, and not good for survival.

"You always say too much, girl!" he would say.

So much about him was a secret, locked away in a steel box. What he did, where he had been, where he was going – it was all kept locked away from prying eyes or ears. There were always whispered conversations with his 'mates' and there was always a reason beyond the reason – a lie behind the lie; a truth behind a veil, a fog of deception.

"If you see Stevie Pierce, don't tell him I was here, see, girl! Don't tell no one, see." It was as if he wanted to become invisible.

***

Invisible, that was how Mary had thought of herself, or how she had wanted to be. *Thump, thump, thump*, the music at the disco blasted their ears, and she had not been able to hear what Paul was saying when he had approached her. He had sat next to her, placing a cocktail on the table, and that simply was how they had met. Mary didn't know why she had agreed to go out that night. Her mum had warned her about the noise, and that it would not be good for the baby. She was three months pregnant. You could not see it, perhaps, although she had already begun to feel a bit bigger, just a tiny bit, although she wasn't sure if she was just imagining it. Her mum had doubted it.

"It's a bit early yet, love. Next few weeks you'll see a difference."

The friends with whom she had gone 'clubbing' had already paired off with 'blokes' they hardly knew, or didn't know at all. Mary wasn't sure. Gyrating closely with a complete stranger, lost in a fathomless, inexplicable, bodily embrace was not something she would now contemplate. She sat alone with a glass of sparkling water. She didn't want to drink alcohol because of the baby. She wished she hadn't come. It wasn't a good idea. She was about to sneak off and get a taxi home – she really wouldn't be missed – but then Paul had come over and sat next to her. At least, suddenly he was there beside her, appearing as if from nowhere to disturb her reverie. She couldn't hear what he was saying, but she did hear him say that his name was Paul. And almost immediately she rather liked him, with that strange knowing. She wasn't sure why. They called it 'chemistry', she knew. It certainly wasn't his conversation.

"It's fucking noisy," she thought she heard him say, although she had her doubts that this was what he had said. It was, she thought, hardly the best chat-up line.

She smiled, or at least she curled her lips into what might pass as a smile. She hadn't asked for the cocktail, and certainly had no intention of drinking it. She played with the little paper and plastic umbrella they put in it, twirling it in her fingers to see the colours, red, green and yellow merge. Also, she wasn't sure what was in the cocktail. He might have put something in it. She had read about it – 'spiking', they called it.

"Thanks, but I'm not drinking alcohol!" she had shouted against the repetitive bass and drum beat.

"What?"

"I said I'm not drinking alcohol!"

"I'm Paul! What's your name?

"What?

"I said, what's your name? Mine's Paul," he had bellowed against the incessant din.

"Mary."

"Do you want to dance, Mary?" Paul asked, half hoping she would say no, as there was nothing he liked less than dancing. There was something moronic, he thought, about his attempts at moving his feet in a fashion anything other than like an elephant plodding through the bush. He tended to gyrate and wave his arms around in what looked like an attempt at an African tribal dance and with little connection to the tempo or rhythm of the music. He felt like an absolute idiot. At best it was a sideways movement, hopping from one foot to another. If the music was slow, the hopping was slower; if it was fast, he simply moved faster. The arm-waving was a vain attempt to compensate for the inadequacy of his foot movement.

"No, thanks," Mary replied reluctantly.

Mary, in contrast to Paul, would have loved to dance. She thought she danced well; everyone said so. With rhythm and timing that matched the suppleness of her body, she moved effortlessly, subtly, the music and movement as one; a seamless picture woven in time. She always enjoyed it. She loved to dance.

"Shall I get you a Coke or lemonade or orange juice?"

"What?"

And so they had met, Paul and Mary; the briefest touch of minds.

Three days later she met him in the street when shopping with her mum. He had run across the street, which was heavy with traffic, to greet them.

"Mary, isn't it?"

"Oh, yes. Hello." Mary had smiled, and Paul had smiled, more with their eyes than their mouths – an intimate, knowing connection.

"We met at the disco. I'm Paul."

"Yes, I know," Mary replied, a little awkwardly now through shyness, briefly breaking the sensual union. Her eyes averted to the ground for an almost imperceptible moment, but then were drawn back to intimacy.

"Well, Mary, do you fancy coming to see a film this evening?"

"Film? What film?"

"No idea, but we could see, couldn't we? What do you say to that?"

What could she say to that? Mary glanced at her mum, who looked bemused by it all. There was something familiar about Paul, her mum had thought. He was rough around the edges, but there was something about him she had recognised. She thought perhaps she knew him, but couldn't quite place where from. She had never met him before as far as she knew, but perhaps he reminded her of someone else. He was immediately familiar. Her eyes met her daughter's glance. It might do Mary some good going to the cinema, she thought, and there wouldn't be too many opportunities after the baby was born. Silence carved a slice through the noise of traffic – not an awkward silence, but a reflective, silence.

"OK." Mary punctured the silence, their eyes locked now in a knowing embrace. A few moments passed, a few beats of the heart, with a soft breeze blowing Mary's hair so she had to hold it away from her eyes, before Paul spoke again, disbelieving of Mary's consent.

"What?" Had he not heard her?

"I said OK, I'll come to see a film." They smiled at each other clumsily. "Whatever film it is!" She added. It didn't, after all, matter what the film would be.

And so they had their first date, Paul and Mary.

Chapter Three: Rose

Today was Friday. Mary could see her mum trudging her way up the winding hill, walking slowly, out of breath and stopping periodically for a short break and transferring the shopping bag from one hand to another, before continuing her slow, painful progress. It would take another twenty minutes before she reached her block, and Mary was worried that the lift wouldn't be working. Her mum had put on a lot of weight, and had heart trouble, but there was something else not right. Mary anxiously watched her mum's laboured progress. She was much worse lately, Mary thought. She always looked, hopefully, for any sign that her mum was better, but she was never better. Often she was worse and showing a progressive deterioration. Her mother wasn't old – fifty-something, approaching sixty, Mary couldn't remember – but she looked old now shuffling up the hill: small steps, each more painful than the one before, her round rosy cheeks puffing and the strain showing on her face. Her hair was grey from the cares of a life of 'making do' and living a day at a time.

Her mother's condition scared Mary. It reminded her of when her father died when she was just a child.

***

"Rose!"

Mary could hear her dad now, calling her mother's name.

"Rose!" he called as he lay in their bed, dying of death, choking up blood and rasping, grasping, each last breath. Mary had once sat with him whilst her mother went to the shops, long ago when she was a child, but the memory etched on her mind. His face had been drawn then – skin and bone almost disappearing into the pillow, and on the bedside table the sweet-smelling liquid that was taking his life as surely as the disease itself. The district nurse had said she'd call by to "make him comfortable". "It's all we can do now," she'd say to her mum. But little Mary had sensed only his pain. She had heard it; she had closed her eyes and wished it away. He had been asleep, a brief respite from the pain and laboured breath. But when he awoke he'd been afraid – not afraid of death itself, but of being without Rose, his partner in life. "Where's your mother?" he'd asked anxiously. His voice hadn't been as weak as Mary had expected, but fear was reflected in his eyes. Mary had run from the room, scared – scarred. It was as if she had done something wrong and been scolded. But of course she hadn't, and nor had he meant to be cross at all. She had never known her dad to be cross, ever, and certainly not with her or her mum. He was the sweetest, kindest man she knew. She missed his laughter and his cuddles so much, when he'd sweep her up in his arms and swing her around before the warmest of embraces.

"Rose!" he would call, impatient, a frightened man sinking. "Rose!"

And Mary would put her hands over her nine-year-old ears, frightened now of the dad she no longer knew. Her mum would stop peeling the potatoes, wipe her hands on her apron and run to his call. There'd be more sweet pink stuff, and then more again, an increasingly futile fight with pain.

"Coming, Dad!" Rose would call back reassuringly as she climbed the stairs, but soon it was over and silence fell, a loud, deafening silence in which the clock on the mantle sounded louder.

Her dad was gone, and that was that. Her mother came back down one day, tiredness in her eyes and tears like raindrops on her cheeks. He was gone, and Mary knew. She had lost her dad.

"Poor Mummy!" she had said. "Poor Mummy!" And that night they had slept together, she and her mum, on the 'put-u-up' sofa in the living room, each believing that they could hear him still as they listened to the deathly hush.

"Such a sweet girl. It's so sad!" the neighbours would say, patting her head. The silence of death and soft, mumbled murmurings of condolence filled the air with the beginnings of sentences fading into nothing.

"He was a lovely man..."

"Lovely man..."

"Never had a bad word for ...."

"He was a lovely man..."

A line of black limousines silently carrying her dad away, shuffling feet on the pavement from neighbours and fellow workmen from the factory, the singing of *Abide with Me,* and he was gone, taken behind the curtain to the sound of an organ.

She didn't know what would happen next. When they went to look at the flowers with their messages of sorrow, she half expected to find her dad waiting for them, putting on his hat and coat ready for them to leave – the warm overcoat that hung on a hook beside the front door along with his trilby hat.

"Come along, Rose. It's time to go, lass," he would say, looking at the watch he proudly wore on his wrist. But not this time. It was his death, and Mary wasn't sure how many deaths you could have. She knew he wasn't coming home.

"The Lord gave, and the Lord hath taken away," the vicar had said in the chapel, where the shuffling feet echoed and you could hear a pin drop, where some cried and others coughed. She waited for him to say that the Lord would give again, but he didn't. And the Lord never did, even when she closed her eyes tightly and hoped it was a dream from which she would wake.

When she returned to school, the headmaster, Mr Hart, said how sorry he was to hear the news of her father's passing. 'Passing' was a funny word, she thought, like a ship in the night.

"It is alright, sir. It was all for the best," she had replied, repeating the comments she had heard at the funeral. "At least he isn't suffering now."

And then, her mother had said, the headmaster had written a letter saying that he was concerned that Mary didn't understand, and suggesting she be sent away for convalescence, so that she "might better adjust". He put her mum in touch with a charity helping sick children take recovery breaks, "a Christian charity who will understand Mary's loss". And so it was: carrying a small brown leather suitcase smelling of mothballs, she was hastily packed off on a bus to join a group of sick children in a faraway place she didn't know, and where she didn't want to be.

But she understood perfectly well all along: her dad was gone, and he wouldn't be coming back, notwithstanding that his overcoat and trilby hat still hung on the hook beside the front door. And it was at the convalescent home that her tears were shed, uncontrollably and inconsolably. She cried every morning when they said the Lord's Prayer, which they insisted on at breakfast: "Our Father who art in heaven". She could get no further with it, and sobbed and sobbed. Her own father was in heaven, and she wished bitterly that he wasn't, and she couldn't understand why "the Lord hath taken away". She wanted him to come through the door in his overcoat and trilby hat and say it was all a mistake. She wanted him to come and take her home. But she knew, of course, that it wasn't a mistake.

"What on earth is the matter with you, child?" the matron had asked.

"My dad's in heaven," Mary tried, and the other children laughed.

"The Lord be praised for that!" the matron responded, never missing an opportunity to administer her Christian belief for the good of all, and adjusting her horn-rimmed half spectacles, grotesquely staring over the top of them at Mary, who was trying so very hard not to cry again.

"Have faith in the Lord Jesus, Mary!" Matron had ministered.

"Yes, miss." But faith about what, Mary wasn't sure.

After a few days they sent Mary home on a bus because she wasn't eating, and they didn't know how to cope with her.

***

The Lord had taken and the Lord wasn't going to give back, Mary reflected, as from the window of their flat she could see a string of white smoke from the crematorium chimney in the distance, another 'passing'. But she could also see her mum making her painfully slow progress up the hill. The hill was a killer. It wasn't so much that the hill was steep, but it was long and the bus stop was at the bottom. Someone in authority had decided to put the bus stop at the bottom of the hill, so the bus could pass the recently disembarked passengers trudging up it, or shoot past them as they ran down the hill to catch it. Sometimes there was a steady stream of young mothers pushing their prams up the hill or down, toddlers in tow and laden with plastic shopping bags. Mary wondered if the authorities had put the bus stop at the bottom to teach them a lesson. The wind blew hard. The wind always blew on the hill, sucking air like a funnel, buffeting this way and that, tearing at umbrellas as though it hated them, grasping them, pulling them out of people's hands, or just simply destroying them with a whistling rage. Paul once said that they should erect a base camp at the bottom so they could prepare for the final climb. "Like conquering fucking Everest!" he had said.

Mary wondered – everyone she knew wondered – why there wasn't a bus stop at the top of the hill. It was as if the council had planned to cut off the estate from the rest of humanity – no way in, no way out. *This is the pits; this is it; this is the end. Here are the ones society forgets,* or would forget with half a chance – a blot on the landscape. Poor, and "Jesus they breed like rabbits". Promiscuous teens sponging off *the social,* dragging their filthy kids around, snotty-nosed, ill-kept and fed on rubbish. *If only they would go away and leave us to pursue our greedy lives.* And that was why the fuckwit, whoever he or she was, had put the bus stop at the bottom of the hill: so that those living at the bottom in their semi-detached houses with a garden wouldn't have to climb up the hill to catch the bus, and they wouldn't have to get off the bus at night so close to the estate.

"You should get up a petition, Mary, you and others on the estate," her mum would often say.

"They don't fucking give a shit, Ma!" was Paul's judgement. "Waste of fucking time!"

'They' were the district council – the council represented by the stiff letters about non-payment of this and that. "We must advise you that you are now three weeks in arrears and unless this is dealt with in the next seven days from the date of this letter we shall be forced to initiate eviction proceedings."

How often it was that Mary and others had received such a letter. There used to be a caretaker, but he had long been replaced by nobody in particular: a number on a torn notice; a number nobody rang because nobody would answer – certainly nobody Mary knew, and probably "another fuckwit" as Paul would say. And now the notice was torn, so that you couldn't see the telephone number anyway. There were tattered and torn notices everywhere prohibiting this, stopping that, do not use this at this time. Nothing ever said what you could do; it was always what you couldn't. And nothing ever worked.

Families were 'put' in Bevin Gardens, rather than 'housed', and Mary had been 'put' in Attlee Tower. It was like a prison sentence, a mark of Cain. Even the bus driver gave a suspicious, condescending look when she asked for a fare to Bevin Gardens, the place where the untouchables lived. And of course the bus didn't really stop at Bevin Gardens.

Mary was not the only teenage mum on the estate or in Attlee Tower. At times it seemed like the estate teemed with single teenage mothers. It was as if it was perfectly natural or part of the culture, and in many ways it was – or at least that was what Mary thought. These teenage mums gathered at the bus stop with their pushchairs carrying their babies like trophies for some, excess baggage for others. Some of the children were fatherless, in the sense that none were ever present, while some mothers had gormless-looking 'men' in tow, who came and went and who may or may not have been the fathers of their messy little brats. Some had more than one child, one after the other, often with different fathers. Even Mary frowned at that. One mistake was enough for her, although hers wasn't a mistake. Fathers floated like bees from flower to flower, carrying their seed as though by accident. It was the sugar they were after: the brief joy of sex with limited cost.

And as for Mary, she didn't know who Michelle's father was. She was the result of a drunken binge with her friends, a quick poke in the dark in the alley next to the pub. The Black Swan, it was, but that was all she remembered. That was all she wanted to remember, and even that was too much.

She'd been sixteen. She remembered little about it, and she never saw the man or boy again, or at least not that she would ever recognise him. She could recall him fondling her breasts, hitching up her skirt, and that was it. She did remember that he called her a 'dirty little bitch' as he thrust once or twice before he was spent, and something like "you love it, don't you!"

But she hadn't loved it; she didn't know what was happening. It was all a fog. She could barely stand up, and when she'd looked for her friends who had been with her, they had gone. They had deserted her. She hadn't done this before; she hadn't been so drunk before. She had been sick, which she remembered, and then he was there, thrusting and calling her a 'dirty little bitch'.

She had been raped, and she felt dirty, always – forever dirty and stained. When she looked in the mirror, she no longer saw the beauty she'd once thought was there. The child had gone, buried deep inside, lost. She felt guilty that she hadn't done enough; she shouldn't have let it happen. She washed, endlessly scrubbing her skin raw, desperate to wipe the stain away and to be clean, but the Lord had given and the Lord had taken away. The child within had died a death, and another child had replaced her: Michelle. For days she had sat in her bedroom, numb, almost believing it hadn't happened. But it had, and even now it would hit her when she least expected, with incessantly restless sleep, recurring dreams from which she would wake in a cold sweat, and an indescribable, penetrating fear.

But sometimes Mary created her own image of Michelle's father, an image in her head. It was an image without stain; how it should have been, and not how it was. She had created him in her mind: how tall he was, the colour of his hair, how strong he was, and how agile. He was serving in the Army – a corporal he was now, perhaps a captain, but she knew her place. He was strong but kind, thoughtful and caring, like her dad had been. He was daring and dashing, and had earned a military medal, fighting in a far-off land. He was intelligent, but down to earth. He could sing; he laughed. He was fun, and he loved Michelle. One day he would come and take them both away while music played like it had in a film she had seen. But it was her own father she imagined, not Michelle's. Her dad it was who had died a death and who would now not reach for his overcoat and trilby hat. But then there was also Paul. But she was never sure about Paul, not yet. Would he stay, or would he leave? Did she want him to stay, or did she want him to leave?

They would live in a small detached house, perhaps a cottage, and he would work as a mechanic in a local garage. Maybe one day they would open a small shop, and she would make a roast on Sundays with peas and gravy and Yorkshire puddings, and with a roly-poly for 'afters' with custard. He would lift Michelle high in the air and swing her around, and she would giggle and laugh and say "Daddy! Daddy!" She wouldn't cry, and she wouldn't wet the bed. They would have a lovely garden full of flowers, he would mow the vast lawn on which they would set up a barbecue, and she would talk to the neighbours over the garden fence. She would write long letters to her mum and aunty, and they would come and stay the night, or stay over for a weekend. And her mum would be well again. All would be well again: her father would be well again, and he wouldn't have died of death. And they wouldn't have patted her on the head and said 'sorry'. She wouldn't have been raped, and she wouldn't be dirty.

Michelle changed Mary's life, but not her destination, or at least in as much as Mary hadn't known what she would do with her life and she still had no idea where she was going. There was no horizon, just day after day, week after week, year on year. Like most of her friends she would have left school anyway and probably worked in a supermarket, just as she had worked in the café in the park, serving teas and buns. Mary's life had changed, because now she wasn't free to do as she pleased. But Michelle was a delight. Nothing else really mattered. Sometimes Mary believed that it was all meant to happen, particularly when she listened to Michelle's incessant babble of half words, stumbled words, rumbled, bumbled words. She adored how she would try to sing along when Mary sang, and the delightful folly of falling around with laughter; stumbling, tumbling.

"Twinkle, twinkle little star, how I wonder what you are." Was it 'what', or 'who'?, she wondered. She could never remember.

Yes, sometimes she felt trapped, but not by Michelle. Michelle was her life; their lives were inextricably interwoven. But this evening she and Paul would be able to go out clubbing or down to the pub because Mum was making her slow, weary way up the hill, as she did at least twice a week and always on Fridays. Always on Fridays, and today was Friday.

Mary's mum was a rock. She had struggled for most of her life, or so it seemed to Mary. She knew how to make do and was always mending this or that, darning socks and patching pants. The one essential in their house had always been the sewing machine, humming away as her mum completed the hems of this or that while listening to the radio. It had been particularly tough after Mary's dad had died and Rose had to work day and night to pay the rent. She was particularly good at sewing, and she took in alteration work, but a trip to the pawnshop was still often necessary with the few bits of jewellery her husband had given her: an engagement ring and a wedding ring. They were worth but a few pounds, but it was enough to tide them over, and sometimes the manager at the Co-Op would arrange vouchers for them to use to buy clothing, which she would pay off weekly.

"We always made do in the old days, Mary; we always made do," her mum would say. There was something reassuring about the way Rose always seemed to be able to find a way round a problem.

It was Mum who had made a set of covers for Mary's sofa and chairs, a suite of two chairs and a sofa that she had bought cheap from a junk shop. The upholstery had long before seen better days. She had found this new stretch material with a pattern on that would "stretch to fit", or so it claimed.

"We'll make them both like they was new, you'll see, Mary love!" her mum had said enthusiastically.

But they didn't look like new, not really. The covers were ill-fitting and homemade-looking, and kept slipping off the arms and baring the dreadful dirty brown of the original upholstery. She had also made the curtains through which Mary now watched her mother as she reached the lamppost just before the entrance to her block. She could see that her mum's face was red. She was breathing with difficulty and she stopped for breath before entering the building.

Mary let the curtain fall back, blotting out the sunlight and plunging the room back into half-darkness. Paul rolled over in bed. He was still asleep, or at least he was in the twilight zone of wakefulness. His tattooed arm lolled sideways on Mary's side of the bed, searching unconsciously for Mary's body – for her warmth, her breasts, and her smooth, soft, silky skin. It found Mary's pillow instead, and he now pulled it towards him and cuddled it as a substitute.

It hadn't been easy for him, Mary thought, smiling as she watched him now. For months she couldn't bear to be touched; couldn't bear to be hugged. Her mum had hugged her as the tears flowed uncontrollably from both of them, but her mum was different.

"I'm sorry, Mum!" she had repeated over and over. "I'm sorry!"

"Hush, it's not your fault, Mary love. It's not your fault!"

"But what are we going to do, Mum?"

"You're going to have that little nipper and we're going to love it to bits, that's what we're going to do, Mary love. That's what we're going to do."

Her mum had been so matter-of-fact and reassuring. It helped Mary cope. But for so long she wouldn't, couldn't, let Paul touch her. Yes, they held hands, even on that first date, but she felt uncomfortable when he put his arms round her shoulders in the cinema. And she knew he would lean over and try to kiss her. What else happened on such dates? She knew he would, and he did, but she couldn't respond. She froze, stiff in the seat. He kissed her tightly closed lips and then backed away. He didn't try again, at least not on that evening.

"I'm sorry!" she said.

"It's OK, girl!" he had said reassuringly.

And when he had walked her home, sharing with her a bag of chips with lots of salt and vinegar, he said it again. "It's OK, girl! It's OK!"

But it wasn't OK. It was not right at all, and she knew he couldn't possibly know why she had rejected him. She couldn't bear to be touched, but it wasn't Paul's fault.

Paul was such an angel when asleep – like a child, Mary thought, in spite of his grunts. He always smiled when he was asleep. She wondered what he dreamed; what he dreamed in the safe world of the never-land. She considered waking him, but decided to let him sleep, at least until she had made a pot of tea for her mum. If they were lucky he wouldn't be awake and they could have a few minutes to chat before waking Michelle and getting her ready for the walk across the park. She heard the familiar clunk of the lift, its doors opening and the hum of its slow ascent. Good, the lift was working!

Mary went to the kitchenette, a small area of the living room separated by a breakfast table. She filled the kettle, plugged it in and switched it on. When she heard the lift doors opening, she rushed to open the door for her mum before she knocked and inadvertently woke Paul.

"Hi, Mum!" she whispered with her finger at her mouth saying "hush".

"Hello, Mary love. I've brought some shopping!" her mum said softly and breathlessly.

"Paul's asleep," Mary whispered, taking the bags.

"Oh, I must sit down, Mary love. That hill kills me, it does!"

It wasn't that Paul would be unpleasant to her mum. He was usually very good to her – he seemed to respect her, the mum he never had to protect him from his father – but he tended to dominate the conversation about this or that. He was always telling everyone else how something should be done, or how they were doing it wrong. He ranted on and on about 'fucking immigrants' and how they were 'taking our jobs' or 'our houses'. And Mary wished they had a job and a house for them to take.

He would stab his finger as though this made his statements more forceful. Mary wondered how they could take 'his job' when he didn't have one, but she wouldn't say so. She also wondered how this could be right when Paul also said that they 'didn't work and were just sponging off the social'. She also wondered who 'they' were. Sometimes they would be 'fucking Pakis'. Anyway, whoever 'they' were, her mum would simply say, 'Yes, you're right there' to whatever it was that Paul was saying.

Mary suspected that her mum didn't really listen to Paul. She would respond by repeating the last bit of Paul's statements.

"They need to fucking send them back where they fucking came from!" he would say.

"Yes", her mum would repeat, lifting her cup and sipping her tea, "where they came from!"

And when her mum had gone, he would say "She's got a lot of sense, your mum!" And Mary would smile. Yes, Mary would muse. The sense not to argue with Paul.

***

Paul grunted and rolled over, half awake and half wondering whether to be awake at all, as he heard the door close and the switch of the kettle. He had a sixth sense for the kettle switch. The low voices of Mary and her mum rumbled through the paper-thin wall. Just as easy to roll over and sleep. But something stirred.

The sun shone a streak of light through the gap in the curtains, forming a strip down the wall and a slash across the bed that dazzled his eyes as he lifted himself out of bed, swivelling his legs over its side and rubbing his fingers through his knotted curly hair.

Shit, he felt bad. His head thumped with the worst of headaches. They had been getting worse over the last few weeks, and there was now barely a day without the torture that felt as though his head was about to burst. His head felt empty, as if his brain had turned to mush, and pain pounded at each beat of his heart.

Mary knew he had been getting headaches, but he hadn't let her know how often, and she had put it down to the booze and the crack. He knew he should see someone about his headaches, but he was too scared to know the truth. He reached over for the pack of tablets on the bedside cabinet. *Take two every four hours. If symptoms persist, see your doctor*, he read as he swallowed two of the pills. But he didn't need to read it. He had read it so many times. "Shit! I'm taking more than that!"

He peeked through the curtain, across the park, squinting at the sun shining in his eyes.

"Fuck me! There's that fucking balloon again!" he muttered, rubbing his eyes and trying to make it disappear. But he could see it way in the distance, hovering and taunting, just above a tree, exactly as it had been a couple of days before. He had seen it then, but not before – not when Mary had pointed to it and said, "Can you see that balloon, Paul?" No, he couldn't see it and he couldn't understand what the fuck she was talking about, although he had seen it, once before. A long time ago when he was small, he had seen it – well, a balloon just like it, hovering above the same fucking tree! But he didn't tell Mary that. That was when he would run to the park to hide from his dad – from his fists and his foul breath, his stinking, fucking foul alcohol-reeking breath. And he saw it now! "Some fucking joker!" he thought. Some drunken bastard with a pea-brain, a late-night reveller who had let it go in the night. There were loads of fucking balloons. Mary talked nonsense about balloons. Silly stuff. *It's just a fucking balloon!* He squinted and it was gone.

***

Bacon! Paul could smell bacon. Mary's mum must have brought some bacon – bacon and eggs for 'brekkie', with fried bread. A fry-up with a mug of tea.

Mary and her mum stopped talking when he entered, still rubbing the sleep from his eyes and running his fingers through the knots in his hair. He hadn't yet washed or brushed his teeth, and he had slipped on his vest and pyjama bottoms or else he would have been naked. Perhaps, Paul thought, they had been talking about him; perhaps not. Women always had their private conversations; hushed voices, a glance, a smile, a frown. In any case, they always talked about nothing of any importance: yap, yap, dress this, top that; "it was as big as this" or "as small as that"; "I asked if they had it in blue but they didn't"; "would you believe it?". Why wouldn't they believe it, for Christ's sake?

Paul squeezed into the kitchenette and gave Mary a brief kiss on the cheek. "Hi, Ma!" He had grown used to calling Mary's mum 'Ma', which Rose considered made them a family, and although she knew Mary wasn't sure what the future held, she regarded Paul like a son-in-law.

"All right, Paul?"

"You're looking great, Ma!" Jesus, she looked awful, he thought! And she did.

"Mum's got another appointment at the hospital, Paul," Mary said, concerned, turning the sizzling bacon.

"And how long has she got to wait for that, then." It wasn't a question, and Paul didn't expect an answer. It was a statement of fact.

"Six months."

Six fucking months! She'd be dead by then. "They're fucking idiots, Ma!"

"They're good doctors at that hospital, Paul. It was on the news – some breakthrough, they called it, about babies," Rose insisted. Rose regarded all hospitals as good and doctors as little short of god-like.

"There are too many fucking babies, Ma!" Paul explained. "That's what the fucking problem is, Ma: too many of the fuckers!" Paul gave a satisfied smile.

"Paul!" Mary remonstrated, turning the bacon onto a plate already laden with two fried eggs and handing it to Paul.

"I'm only saying how it is, Mary. I mean, take a fucking look at this fucking estate!" Paul eyed the two rashers on his plate, squeezing the ketchup – slurp, and slurp. "Anyhow, what the fuck have babies got to do with your appointment, Ma?"

"Nothing, I suppose."

"It ain't got nothing to do with it, Ma! And that's a fact! And I'll tell you another thing too!" Paul continued, prodding the air with his knife. "All the fuckers on this estate can breed like rabbits, but them middle-class wankers can't fucking do it so they have to fucking well do it in a fucking dish!"

"Test tube," Mary corrected. Paul grunted.

"They're called 'test-tube babies'," Mary explained.

"I know what they're fucking called!"

They laughed, but their laughter was interrupted by a knocking at the door, soft at first, and barely audible, then louder now, and louder still, followed by the rasping bell.

"That'll be Shaker," Paul said, with a guilty glance at Mary.

"Jesus, Paul, not today! I thought we were going out!"

"We are, girl. It's only Shaker, for Christ's sake!"

Only Shaker... Shaker was Mickey Duff, and he was 'Shaker' because he shook. He always shook, uncontrollably. He had always shaken uncontrollably. He had some kind of neurological problem, Paul had said, from birth.

The rasping bell and the knocking moved to a crescendo – *bang, bang, rasp, rasp* – until eventually Paul opened the door.

"Fucking hell, Shaker, don't break the fucking door down!"

"All right, Mickey?" Mary asked with a smile. She couldn't be cross with Shaker, poor Shaker who shook, and she never called him Shaker. His name was Mickey and she thought calling him Shaker because he shook was cruel.

Shaker nodded. Well, he always nodded, but Mary knew that this was a nodding nod.

"You want a tea, Mickey? We just made it fresh," she added, pouring four mugs and adding milk and loads of sugar for Shaker. Shaker liked sugar; lots of sugar. Once she had let him spoon his own sugar, but it went all over the place. Now she always put it in for him.

Shaker was tall and gangly. Well, he wasn't really that tall. He just looked tall because he was thin. He dragged his left leg, which was lifeless – or at least, it had a life of its own: an uncontrollable life, as though it was always fighting to be left behind or as if it belonged to a different body. Mary watched as he leaned forward to sip his tea, cupping his hands round the warm mug but not lifting it. He tilted the mug and slurped the tea. It was as if the soothing warmth calmed him, and just for an instant – a moment, a sip – he didn't shake. *If only life was an endless cup of tea, Shaker*, Mary thought. He looked up and smiled a large toothy smile, his head bobbing and weaving as if performing a dance.

Paul had known Shaker since they were at school, and they'd been inseparable since they were fourteen. Shaker had changed his life, and he felt he owed Shaker, although Shaker never knew it. Paul was Shaker's friend; Paul was Shaker's only friend. Mary had to put up with Shaker wherever they went. When they went to the cinema, Shaker was there, shaking. She had given up trying to shake Shaker – he was unshakable, and so she had resigned herself to him. He was an attachment, an appendage, a third person in their relationship, but she did like him. She felt comfortable with him. He was part of their family now; she'd even give him a hug occasionally, which Shaker loved.

It was anger that had made Shaker Paul's friend – anger and fate, and a chance meeting. The day they'd met, Paul was running from his dad, from another beating. He ran to the park as always – ran and ran, faster and faster, as though he could go on running until he was far away and lost, never to find his way back. But he ran into Jacky Spence, 'Bully' Spence.

Shaker had been walking home across the park from the 'special needs' class he attended after school. It wasn't unusual that he was the target for jokes and bullying. Sometimes the cruelty of other children knew no bounds. They would taunt him, tease him, and generally make his life a misery on a daily basis. He wasn't the only victim by any means. The bullies had a sixth sense for the vulnerable and the sensitive. Sometimes the bullied became the bullies. It was often the art of survival, seeking acceptance from others by becoming one of the group.

Bully Spence and his mates had surrounded Shaker, taunting him, pushing him and kicking him. They had taken his bag and spilled its contents – books, papers, pens and pencils – and stamped on them. They were laughing, and Shaker was laughing, but Shaker was crying too, a hybrid of crying and laughing.

Without thinking, in his rage, Paul had leaped on Bully Spence, knocking him to the ground and proceeded to give him a sound beating, his fists pummelling Bully's face. So fast did he act that the others barely had a chance to react; they were stunned and ran off.

Paul was so fierce, so angry, that all he saw was his father, and he punched and punched. And he would have gone on punching if Shaker hadn't tried to pull him off.

"No! No! No!" Shaker cried in his strange shaking voice. "That's enough!"

When Paul let Bully up, the boy ran off crying, and that day changed Paul's life forever. It was that day the spring was wound so tight. Within days his reputation spread: he had beaten up Bully Spence, and Bully Spence was never the same again. Paul was never the same either. Nobody touched him, and nobody touched Shaker. It changed his life, because from that day he was never bullied, at least not while Paul was around.

***

Toast with jam, raspberry jam, was Shaker's favourite with a mug of tea.

"You want some toast, Mickey?"

Thought she would never ask! "Yes, please!" Shaker nodded, looking for the raspberry jam pot. Marmalade! Only marmalade!

"You got no raspberry?"

His mum always gave him raspberry jam. It was his favourite. He liked damson jam too, which his mum would make in jars that she kept in the larder. He was disappointed. But that is what life was like: "full of shit", as Paul would say. He plunged the spoon in the jar, shaking, and dished a load of thick marmalade onto his toast, shaking.

Paul looked down from the kitchenette window to see if Bully Spence was waiting. He saw him across the road leaning on a burned-out car. He glanced up, sensing Paul was there. He waved and looked at his watch, pointing to it. It was late, and there wasn't much time left if they were to get the job done. Paul waved and turned back to see Shaker take a bite of toast with the thickest layer of marmalade – so thick that it oozed over the side, dripping onto the table. Shaker caught Paul's glance and smiled, a dollop of marmalade stuck on the end of his nose.

"Um… look, girl. I know I said we was going out today, but..." Paul began sheepishly.

"Jesus, Paul!"

"Well, fuck me, a job has come up see and… well."

"OK, fucking go to your fucking job, then. See if I care!" Mary knew he wouldn't be coming with them as soon as she saw Shaker; she was already resigned to that. Sometimes Shaker was such bad news! But she would enjoy a walk in the park with her mum and Michelle, just the three of them.

"Is there any money in it, Paul?" Mary's mum asked, with a disapproving glance at Mary for her foul language.

"Could be, Ma. There could be," Paul smiled.

"Well, Mary, you could do with a bit of extra, love."

"Is it with that Bully Spence?" Mary asked suspiciously; anxiously. She knew what a job with Bully Spence would mean: trouble. Always trouble with Bully Spence.

Chapter Four: Candyfloss and Butterflies

"Candyfloss." Rose broke the silence as they sat on the bench in the shade of the tall ash tree, which provided at least some respite from the heat of the midday sun.

"What, Mum?"

"Candyfloss!"

"Yes, Mum. Candyfloss." Mary had no idea what her mum was referring to. What she knew was that her mum often started conversations by reference to something she recalled: an object, a taste, a feeling.

"We used to come here regular when we was kids!" Rose continued, as if this was itself an explanation.

"Yes, Mum. We did when we was kids too." Father to son, mother to mother, generation to generation, Mary reflected. The boys played cricket; the girls played rounders.

"Yes, but it ain't like the old days. Not now, it ain't!" Rose smiled, remembering the old days, when she was a happy child playing in the park with her friends. "This bench was here then too, you know," she added, patting the wooden bench with its carved names. "And we used to have candyfloss."

"Is your ice-cream good, Mum?" Mary asked, before rolling her tongue round the rim of her own delectable vanilla and raspberry cornet.

"Mmm, it's lovely!"

The sun shone without a cloud in the sky. It was one of those balmy days – hot, very hot – and Rose's ice-cream melted quicker than she could lick it, even though they were in the shade. She had to hold it out so that it wouldn't drip onto her coat, which it had done already in at least two places that Mary could see.

"And toffee apples! Oh, they was lovely, the toffee apples! Nice and crisp toffee on the outside and bitter-sweet in the middle."

"Yes, Mum." Mary tried to think what bitter-sweet tasted like, but she thought she understood. It was a taste she liked too: sweet with a slightly bitter taste that lingers in the mouth. A bit like Paul, she mused, except perhaps the other way around. Paul was, she considered, sweet on the inside, particularly when asleep.

"There used to be a fun fair here, you know, when we was kids. It used to come every year. Your dad and I did most of our courting here. Of course, we didn't have much money to do much else in them days."

"We don't have much money now, either, Mum!" And that, Mary thought, was an understatement.

"That's true, Mary love. That's true."

They sat for a while concentrating on eating their ice-creams, until again it was Rose who broke the silence. "He was such a handsome man, your dad, and so considerate. He used to brush this bench with his hanky before he would allow me to sit down on it. Proper gentleman, he was!"

Mary glanced at her mum, thinking of her dad and what she remembered about him. Sometimes she could see him, what he was like, but mostly his face had become a distant haze, and if she didn't have the photograph to look at, she wondered whether she would remember at all. She did remember a thin face with a fag in its mouth, and large eyes – once alive, now dead – but it was all in a mist. She struggled hard for each feature, trying to make him real again – his eyes, his nose, the sound of his voice – but just as he seemed to appear, he disappeared without form. She didn't know who the other two men in the picture were, but she remembered that they were there, one sitting on the floor, a small man with a smile. Her mum had said they'd all been on an outing to the seaside. She vaguely remembered, with ice-cream then too.

"Your throne is ready, ma'am, he used to say, and then he'd bow and I would sit down. Oh, he was such a funny man, your dad!"

A funny man, Mary thought. Did she remember him as 'funny'? She remembered his pain and him calling out. But, yes, he was 'fun', like on the trip to the seaside, swinging her around and singing funny songs. The tune echoed in her mind now: *Oh, I do like to be beside the seaside. Oh, I do like to be beside the sea!* She inadvertently hummed the tune, softly.

"What was that, love? I didn't hear you."

"Nothing, Mum. Nothing really. Just a song."

"Your dad liked a good song."

They'd bring a transistor radio to listen to the chart-toppers on Radio Luxemburg – a red radio with a light-brown leather holder with a strap and a big wheel to dial up the stations. He'd saved up his wages to buy it, and they loved tuning in to the foreign channels too, the exotic places they couldn't go, far-off places – or at least they'd seemed far-off in those days. Now they were just a short hop away on a plane for a weekend, and full of people: crowded, uncomfortable, with rip-off hotels and silly people lying in the sun when they could just as easily be here, lying in the sun.

"Of course, you was conceived here too, Mary love."

Mary smiled an embarrassed smile, but only because she didn't really know how else to react. As if it was important where she was conceived! And then she thought of Michelle and the seedy way her own daughter was conceived: down an alley, in the dark, with a bloke she didn't know.

She'd never rejected Michelle. She'd loved her almost from the moment she was born, from the moment she first poked her tongue out and smiled. Michelle would mimic every facial movement: when Mary poked out her tongue, baby Michelle followed suit; when Mary smiled, Baby smiled. Michelle had opened her eyes to the world one at a time: first the left, and then the right eye had opened, saying hello to the world. Mary was entranced. Baby and mother were entranced, enchanted, a touching of minds in a new world, and they had been together on an expedition of discovery ever since. But sometimes, in the darkest moments, she would recoil from the thought that part of the bastard that raped her was there, in her baby; an insidious seed lurking deep inside, forever haunting. She would feel a coldness, a deep sinking, a part torn from her soul, and an ugliness so profound that she struggled to breathe. It would be for just a fleeting moment when she caught a glimpse of him in Michelle's eyes, as though he was there looking at her, and in the colour of her hair – fair where her own was dark. And Michelle would respond as though she sensed her mother's feeling. Remorseful, Mary would kiss her and say sorry.

"Now, how do you know that, Mum? You can't know for sure!"
"Oh, yes, I can, love!" It was her mum's turn to smile. It was a real smile, almost a chuckle – a chuckle turning into a cough. It often turned into a cough – a rasping, hacking cough that left her breathless, but not this time. "It was the only place we'd done it!"
Mary laughed. They both laughed, and Mary gave her mum a hug. And Michelle laughed too, although she didn't know why, and her ice-cream fell out of the cornet onto her lap. Within moments she was crying, holding the empty cornet in disbelief. Another moment in the journey together.
Mary was an only child, and they'd had her late, although it wasn't for want of trying. They'd wanted to start a family so much, but it just didn't happen. "It'll be alright. You'll see, pet!" Jo would say assuredly, forever an optimist. But in truth they had all but given up. A committed socialist, Jo had thrown himself into trade-union activity at the factory and played tuba in the brass band. They were not destined, Rose had thought, to be blessed with children. They'd never blamed each other, and it had never affected the bond between them. It was just how it was. They still had each other; they still loved each other, with an undying

love as strong as the day it flickered into being the evening they met at one of the factory socials. Mary was their little miracle.

"There were houses all along over there," Rose mused, pointing across to the estate, her wizened finger marking out the line where the houses had been. "They pulled them down to build the flats."

Mary wiped the ice-cream from her daughter's lap with a piece of tissue, and took out another to wipe her face.

"We used to live in one of them houses too. It was where I was born – number 53 Latimer Street, it was. There were six of us in that tiny terraced house: my mum and dad, your gran and grandpa – I don't suppose you remember much about them, 'cause they died soon after you was born – and me and my three brothers. We all lived in that house, on top of each other, but we was all happy, Mary love. We was all happy."

Mary played with the buttons on Michelle's cardigan, patiently listening to her mum.

"We had a little garden at the back. Well, it wasn't much of a garden, really. It was really where we put the bins. But Dad made it into a garden, with roses growing round a trellis. He loved roses, did our dad. He would have loved to have had a big garden. But we could play in the street in them days. I remember when your uncle Cedric had one of those little pedal cars that you sat in and pedalled it along. Of course, it only had three wheels. One was missing 'cause Dad had found it on a rubbish tip and brought it home and cleaned it up for Cedric, but he never found another wheel, and your uncle Cedric had to lean over on one side to keep it from tipping over! But he used to race that car up and down the street. One day he knocked over Mrs Braithwaite's milk bottles and everyone came out to see what the fuss was about. They rolled all over the place, those milk bottles, and Mrs Braithwaite was chasing Cedric down the street with a broom. It was ever so funny, Mary love! He was pedalling so fast, and you could see his knees bobbing up and down! Well, of course, she caught up with him in the end and pulled him out by the cars and marched him back to see Dad. Of course, our dad found it funny too, but he didn't let Mrs Braithwaite know that. 'How many times have I told you?' he said to Cedric. 'Now get upstairs this minute and I don't want to hear another word!' And he added, 'I'll see to it, Mrs Braithwaite, rest assured of that!' And it was about as much trouble you ever got into in them days."

Mary opened a bar of chocolate that she remembered she had in her bag, meticulously broke it, and handed pieces to her mum and to Michelle, who had stopped crying.

"We used to get candyfloss from the fun fair. There was a fun fair came every year when we was kids." Rose sighed. "It's long gone now, though."

"Time we started back, Mum!" Mary started to get up, collecting the paper bags together and putting them in the back of the pushchair. She had heard her mum's story so many times. It wasn't that she was impatient with her, but they had to get back.

"We used to feel safe in them days. People looked after you in the street. 'All for one, and one for all,' your dad used to say. Nowadays they look the other way, don't want to be involved. Nobody wants to know anymore."

"Too scared, Mum. It's different now, and as Paul says, you can't trust no one," Mary said knowingly.

"Everyone knew each other, see! They all worked at the factory. Well, all the men did, and when they closed the factory there was such a lot of hardship. 'Mass unemployment', they called it, or 'restructuring', and people had to move away to find work."

Rose fell silent, reflecting on how so much had changed, and a life passed. She wondered where they had all gone, her friends, what they were doing, whether they'd had families, how many children they'd had and what they were doing.

"Well, we felt safe. At least we did until little Annie went missing. Poor little Annie! She was such a sweet girl. We was such good friends, Annie and me. We did all sorts together and always shared our sweets at school. She was like a sister, really, and we was always in and out of each other's houses. We was playing that day she went missing. We thought she'd gone home, see. And she was always hiding away and stuff like that. Always playing games, was Annie. But we shouldn't have left her, Mary. We shouldn't have."

Annie, Annie. Always back to Annie. Mary waited patiently, for she had heard the story time and again, and she stood silently, lovingly running her fingers through Michelle's silky-soft hair, before she asked, "Did they ever find out who did it, Mum?"

"No, Mary love. Not to this day, they haven't. But then they never found her, see? I expect they stopped looking a long time ago. It was all such a long time ago, I suppose nobody round here remembers. "

But Rose remembered: an interminable loss; an irremediable wound. Annie and Rose had been inseparable. They'd sat next to each other at school, and they played with each other in the playground, yes, but their minds were one. Each could feel the pain, the likes, the fears, and the excitement of the other. Yet they couldn't have been more different: Annie the bold tomboy, Rose the fairy on the cake. Annie the bold, intrepidly taking her torch into the dark, and Rose, cautiously standing back. Annie the derring-do, Rose the 'must not'.

"Come on, Rose!" Annie would cry, clambering over a garden fence to 'scrump' apples from a tree.

"We'll get caught, Annie, and then what?"

And sometimes they did get caught, and the 'then what' was a good ticking-off. But the sky didn't fall in on them, and Annie was simply determined not to be caught again. Rough and tumble, was Annie, yet she could dance like a ballerina. She could clamber up a tree, but she loved to dance, her body simply floating on air.

Rose had loved country-dancing at school. She loved the rhythms; she loved the twirls as they'd go round and round in circles, first this way and then reverse. The boys would be shy. It was one of the rare activities they did together, the boys and girls. But Charlie, she remembered, had liked to dance.

Sometimes the teacher would play the piano; sometimes there would be music from the radio or a record – a record that would click and hiss from the scratches, and the needle would sometimes get stuck in a groove and the music would repeat. But it wasn't the same when Annie had gone. They had smiled and laughed with joy as they linked arms and twirled, round and round, but Annie had gone and it wasn't the same.

Rose would often sit on this same bench. It brought a closeness to Annie, as if it was Annie's bench. Rose would sit in silence, and sometimes, when she closed her eyes, when she could shut out the clutter of daily noise, she would hear Annie's voice, or perhaps a giggle – the sound of the ever-present laughter of Annie.

"It was the day the school burned down when she went missing. That's why we were playing in the park!" Rose recalled.

"I know, Mum," Mary replied gently, sensing her mum's pain.

A butterfly danced, flapping its wings. Down it came, and landed on Michelle's head. Mary put a cupped hand towards it, and it climbed onto her thumb, briefly, gently, gently moving its wings, slowly, as if warming them in the sun. Mary felt the tickle of its legs on her skin, gently clinging.

"Annie was like a butterfly," Rose remarked. "Ever so gentle, she was, dancing all the time and flapping her wings."

Up and down, the butterfly slowly moved its wings, turning a circle on Mary's thumb.

"There was a bloke on the telly I heard once," Rose mused, "who said that when a butterfly flaps its wings it causes changes all over the world and for all time."

"Sounds daft to me, Mum." Mary didn't really think it was daft. In fact she rather liked the idea, but it was getting late and they needed to get back.

"Annie was like that," Rose continued, reflectively.

"Like what, Mum?"

"When she flapped her wings, like a butterfly, she was. Everything changed when she flapped her wings."

Mary thought it odd that Annie should have wings, but she'd learned that nothing was strange about Annie.

A little breeze lightened the air, brushing against her cheek. The butterfly flew off, weaving its course into the trees. And just briefly a few leaves scattered on the path, whipped into the air, to descend softly back to the ground.

Chapter Six: The Making of Bully Spence

Riding his bicycle recklessly up and down the path by the lake wielding a stick as a sword, Bully Spence at ten years old was a knight on a charger, riding and slashing at the tulips, knocking their heads off. Some days he was a king holding court with his slaves and serfs, on others he was a gangster, head of the Mafia, or the leader of a platoon. These were the games he liked to play: always on top with others doing his bidding. Bully Spence and his merry gang. Bully Spence was big, but not overweight. He had always been big. He was a big baby, causing his mum great pain when he was born, about which she never tired of telling him and for which she never forgave him.

"I should have closed my legs tight when you was born, such trouble you've been. Snuffed you out at birth, I should have!"

The birth was difficult, and she had to go into hospital. The pain of his birth was at the heart of it, followed by a deep depression from which his mum had never recovered as far as her son was concerned. So many tears she shed, like an incessant mourning. Her husband and children she had loved so much appeared now as strangers, distant beings she did not know, and the happy days of housy-housy were gone, never to return. A dark descended; a darkness so black that barely a shred of light could penetrate, but she could not explain; she could not tell how she felt. Bully felt she hated him, and for the most part she did. There were times when she tried, and sometimes she tried so very hard to cuddle him, to love him, to feel for him, but it just wouldn't come. There was no bonding, just a loathing. He might have been someone else's child. Often she wondered if he was a mistaken substitution, but the pain of his birth had been real enough.

His sisters were big too, when they were born, and his brother. Bully wasn't an only child, but he was at best a lonely one. Bully was a mistake – he shouldn't have happened, and his mum (and dad) never quite got over it. "That boy will be the death of me, the ungrateful brat!"

Bully's mum would have very little to do with him. She often left him in the care of his sisters, who were barely old enough to look after themselves and were encouraged to mistreat him. Sometimes they would; often they wouldn't. Sometimes they showed an instinctive caring for a younger brother and would mother him like a doll substitute. But some days – the bad days, the blue days – egged on by their mother, they would show their worst vindictive instincts.

"Don't you go giving him no treats! He don't deserve it," their mother would say. "And if he's naughty I'll give him a thrashing, you see if I don't." And a thrashing she would give, his screams echoing through the house. The neighbours turned a blind eye and a deaf ear. It wasn't as if he was the only child to receive a thrashing, but the thrashing wasn't the worst to bear: worst was the deprivation and rejection, emotions held like strips of paper to be torn at will, and the many lonely hours spent in his room – a room cold with the stark reality of his existence. There was a vacuum where there should have been love, cold where there should have been warmth, and nothing where there should have been something: a tangible toy denoting love, affection, want and need. He had the barest cupboard for his clothes, and the thinnest blanket against the winter cold.

When his father was away it was worse, much worse, and if his father had half an inkling of what went on, he didn't show it. He never said, but for an occasional remonstrance of, "Give the boy a chance!" But she never did.

Bully's father was away a lot, a long-distance truck driver hauling goods all over Europe. Making trips over thousands of miles, he would be away sometimes for days. Bully fantasised about his dad. When he was home he took Bully for boxing lessons, and Bully got good – too good, so Bully claimed. When he was older he tried to turn professional, but "nobody would fight me, see, because I was too good!" he once told Shaker. He'd "been on the telly with that fight when I won the trophy", and it looked as if he would have a great career ahead as a fighter. Little or none of this was true. Bully exaggerated everything.

But Bully believed in the fragment of truth, sufficient as a seed that could grow into a bigger tree. And when Bully talked, he could grow tall and feel good for a moment, and that was the problem for Bully. A light of dawn would come: reality would probe deep into his soul, a festering sore. Rejection, failure, rejection, anger, frustration, a hurt... a seed sufficient to grow into a bigger tree, an inner wail of a lost creature, someone who was but isn't, and someone who should have been but isn't. Someone who could but can't. Someone rejected.

"I should have closed my legs tight when you was born, such trouble you've been. Snuffed you out at birth, I should have!"

And if it was true, Shaker couldn't remember it, not that Shaker took much interest in boxing. He smiled at Bully and shook his head. It could have been true, for all he knew. Bully was big, and he guessed that made a difference. It wasn't that he had much skill – he was a cumbersome, lumbering giant – but he could probably punch with power, and according to one of Bully's mates, the managers of up-and coming-boxers, those with agility and skill, wouldn't risk their boys in the ring with him. "They wouldn't fight me, see? 'Cause I had a punch." And so he had been sidelined, or so he said – a never-has-been of the boxing world.

"He's been nothing but trouble for me, that boy!"

"Give the boy a chance!" his father would say.

"It's all very well for you. You're not here most of the time to put up with him. Ungrateful! That is what he is! He needs teaching a lesson on how to behave!"

"Just give the boy a chance, that's all I'm saying."

"We never had no trouble with the others. Good as gold, they was. Nobody can say I'm not a good mother. There's something not right with him, not right in the head. Always has been. I told you, but you wouldn't listen. Gives me the creeps, he does."

Bully's dad had wanted him to be successful in boxing. He thought it was something the boy could do. It wasn't that his boxing failure affected Bully too much, but it affected his father, who had dreamed of his son being the British heavyweight champion, if not the heavyweight champion of the world. That much, at least, Shaker knew to be true. He once heard Bully's dad talking about it. It was all a dream, of course – a pipe dream, so far from the real world that it didn't make sense, and there was little that Bully could do to live up to his father's expectations. In his dreams he was the hero his dad wanted; in reality he was the failure his dad expected.

But his dad wasn't annoyed. He seemed to understand, at least sometimes. He'd come into his room and try to talk to him, reasoning, "You mustn't blame your mother too much, son. She does her best for us all!"

And Bully tried hard not to blame his mother. He tried to understand. He had tried to please his mother so many times, but always came the rejection. His dad didn't understand. His mother detested him, and he didn't know why.

"You away again tomorrow, then, Dad?"

"Yes, son, right across France and into Italy."

"Maybe I could come with you, Dad?"

"One day, son, perhaps. One day. We'll have to see." But 'one day' never came.

And then he'd shadow-box him, ducking and weaving and gently 'punching' his stomach. "Keep your guard up, son. Always keep your guard up."

And when his dad left the room, he heard his mum: "Did you tell him? Did you give him what-for? He'll be the death of me, that boy. He never shows gratitude, just sits and sulks. And I'm fed up with his lies. I won't put up with it. Something wrong with him; I've told you."

"Give it a rest, woman. I told him, right?"

"Bully's a fucking lying prat!" Paul had told Shaker, although they hung out together and Shaker never understood why.

The truth was that Bully wasn't a good boxer. He won one school-boy amateur boxing tournament by his sheer power and a lot of luck, and as a professional he wouldn't have lasted a round; they would have run rings around him. As for the story, you paid your money and took your choice of truth or fiction. The smallest pebble became a rock; a grain of sand in a desert became a dune. Humming a pop tune made him a star. At the cinema he was a famous movie mogul, a gangster, a pirate, a submariner, a soldier or sailor. He was all these things and none. The one thing Bully had was imagination.

Bully Spence was also a persistent liar. At best he lived in a fantasy world – a world in which his father could just as readily be a war hero, single-handedly fighting off a platoon of Nazi soldiers during the war or an intelligence officer working undercover for the security services, which was why he was away such a lot on secret missions behind the Iron Curtain.

His father had been a pilot, a first officer in the Navy and a submariner, and while he was doing all that he had parachuted behind enemy lines as a marine. Such stories had always come readily to Bully Spence, as readily now as when he was a boy. And everyone he knew was aware that his father wasn't born until the war with Germany was over, and apart from a stint in national service when he was stationed in Germany, he certainly hadn't got close to being a marine. He drove trucks; he drove them in the Army and then he drove them when he left it, and he would probably always drive trucks. Arthur Spence didn't amount to much at all, and nor was it likely that his youngest son would either.

The other thing Shaker knew about Bully's dad was that he kept an allotment where he grew cabbages and carrots and other such vegetables. Once when they were kids, he and Bully had helped pick the cabbages and tomatoes, placing them in two big cardboard boxes. Bully's dad had patted Shaker on the head and given him two of the cabbages to take home for his mum, but his mum had thrown them straight into the bin because they were rotten and eaten by caterpillars. "What a bloody cheek!" she had said, "and you working so hard for him." And Shaker had shook. "I'll not have you going round there again!" she had said, and Shaker never did.

Even before Bully left school, he had drifted into the sticky clutches of Steven Pierce. Pierce was a local villain and fence – a small-time crook at the periphery of organised crime. Just as Bully became his gofer, so Pierce was the gofer for the bigger fish. It gave Bully a sense of importance. Bully was Pierce's poodle, and Pierce also liked young boys. What Bully failed to get from his mum and dad, he thought he got from Pierce: a father figure, someone to look up to and someone who in turn gave him respect, attention, self-worth, and a sense of being wanted.

At first it was uncomfortable, the touching. He'd gone into Pierce's office at the back of his night club. Pierce was rarely alone; he usually had two or three gofers with him, and two big bouncers for protection.

"Did you do that errand for me, Spence?"

"Yes, Mr Pierce."

"Good boy."

Good boy. Nobody had called him that. Sometimes his dad did, but he was away. *Good boy.* It made him feel good; a warm feeling deep inside. It made him want to please, to get more praise. It made him want to be *a good boy*.

"Wait outside until I call you!" Pierce had instructed his henchmen, who quietly left the room, leaving him and Bully alone.

"Are you going to please me, Spence?"

"Yes, Mr Pierce."

Bully was Mr Pierce's *good boy* for almost a year. Pierce made him feel special, and gave him a gold necklace and a ring. The fingers of both Pierce's hands were adorned with gold, and he always wore a gold necklace with a large pendant that Bully saw on his lean, hairy chest when he removed his shirt. Bully pleased Mr Pierce several times a week, but then the "come and see me tomorrow" became "I'll call you if I need you". And then one day when he was calling after running an errand, Pierce had another young boy in his office, slender and younger and more boyish. It was Bully's turn to wait discreetly outside with the bouncers. Bully was hurt, and found it difficult to control his jealousy, frustration and rejection. He was particularly hurt because being Pierce's *good boy* had been the first time he had felt wanted. It was impossible to understand, and resulted in an inner rage – a sense of loss. Yes, a sense of loss. Something had been taken away, and like a drug he had become dependent on it. He needed it; he was addicted to it.

But Pierce didn't ignore or abandon Bully, and gave him more jobs to do. He trusted him, and Bully's addiction made him easy to manipulate, obedient without question.

"You do right by me, Spence, and I'll see you all right. Understand?"

"Yes, Mr Pierce."

"Good boy."

He could still be a good boy.

It wasn't that he ever really liked Pierce's sexual advances; he just got used to them. It became easier, more natural, and he got pleasure from giving pleasure. At first it made him feel awkward, but he had never felt it was wrong. Pierce looked after him. Messing with Bully Spence meant messing with Pierce, and there were few around who would do that. Nor did he find it difficult when Pierce introduced him to his accountant, an elderly, posh-speaking Jewish man. The conversation was short and to the point.

"This is my accountant, Spence. I want you to be a good boy and please him."

"Yes, Mr Pierce."

He pleased the old man on many occasions, and there were others too. He learned not to speak – just to do as he was told and to relax. It made him popular. Bully got passed around, and the more he was used, the more he had that warm feeling of being wanted and the more it eased the loss and peeled away the pain. Without it, he felt out of control, unable to contain his anger at his mother's rejection.

Paul didn't like Spence much, yet they always seemed to hang out. Since the beating Paul had given him when they were at school, Spence had a guarded respect for Paul. Yet although he was wary of him, Bully always seemed to pull Paul into one scheme or another with a job here, a job there. Mostly they were sufficiently on the right side of the law: cash-in-hand jobs, a delivery, a car needing doing up without too many questions asked. Paul asked few questions; it was best to just get on and do it and get the money. Usually Pierce was involved in some way or other, but usually at a distance. Pierce knew how to keep just one step removed from any job, legal or otherwise; they would never find his fingerprints should anything go wrong. "You do right by me, Spence, and I'll always see you right, OK?"

"I've got a job, Paul, if you're interested. Good money in it," Bully would say.

"What's it worth?"

"Hundred up front. Double if it goes OK."

It was all done with a nod a wink and an, "I'll see you're OK."

***

Mary didn't like Bully Spence either. He made her nervous; he was shifty and she sensed in him a deviousness. He never looked her in the eye, and always had his hands in his pockets – not casually, but as though he was hiding something: a knife or other such sinister concealment. His black, matted hair was always greasy, and he sweated a lot. He told tall stories that she found embarrassing because they were such obvious fantasies. She hated having to say 'yes' and 'that's interesting' in order to avoid suggesting he was a liar.

He put her on edge – she spilled things, she dropped things, she forgot things, and she let things boil over on the stove. Bully Spence was trouble, and she was disappointed that he was in the flat with Paul when she and her mum returned from their walk.

"What's the problem, Paul?" she asked, sensing his agitation.

"Problem? No problem. What makes you say that?" Paul replied, glancing shiftily at Bully.

Mary looked at Bully and then at Paul as if to say: "That's why!"

Bully grinned – or perhaps it was a sneer. Whichever it was, it wasn't particularly pleasant. He swept his matted hair back from his eyes. Bully had made a bad first impression, and there was nothing he could do now to redeem himself. His awkwardness reflected the fact that she made him feel awkward. *Silly cow!* he thought, leering at her and fantasising about how he would cut her into pieces with a chainsaw after drilling her eyes out with a power drill. *Silly bitch. I'll teach you a lesson!* He wondered what it was that Paul saw in her. He must be mad, or else he got his leg over. She was a bit of slag, the dirty cow, and that filthy little girl of hers always had jam on her face and shit on her hands. But she drove Bully mad sexually: her silky-soft thighs and her breasts, he could only imagine, accentuated by the tightness of her jumpers. Yes, he thought, it was the sex that Paul was attracted to.

"All right then, Mary?" he asked clumsily. "Me and Paul was planning to watch some footie on the telly and drink a few beers."

Mary looked daggers at Paul. Paul looked sheepishly at the floor.

Bully liked girls to be sluts and objects of sexual gratification – items to be used and disposed of. Then he could handle them. Or, he saw his mother in all of them. His relationship with them had to be purely physical – without love and without affection – or he couldn't handle it. He couldn't face the fear of rejection.

"You get that work done then, Paul?" her mum asked, seeking to defuse Mary's anger. She didn't want a row, and she sensed her daughter's simmering mood and her disappointment.

"What work, Ma?" Paul replied, before realising his mistake. "Oh yes, Ma, we got that done early, see, so we thought we'd watch the footie, as Bully says."

"So what match is it, then?" Mary asked, knowing Paul would have no idea.

"Man United!" Bully responded before Paul made a hash of it. "They're playing Chelsea." And so they were, but Paul hadn't known that. He looked at Bully as if to say "great one, Bully", before returning to Mary.

"Yeah, Man United and Chelsea," he echoed.

Mary wondered why Bully's hair was always so greasy. It reminded her of the sheen of the greased hair of 1950s movie stars. She wondered what happened in hot weather: melting grease running down their necks and foreheads. Bully's hair must be naturally greasy; she wondered if he ever washed it.

Mary had put the kettle on, and now spooned out instant coffee from a tin. She even prepared a mug for Bully.

"You out of teabags, Mary love?" her mum asked.

Mary reached up into the cupboard for a teabag. Bully watched her short skirt rise up, revealing her firm thighs. She had great legs, he thought – sexy, real sexy and what a slut she had been to have a nipper and not know the father! Paul was a jammy bastard, but maybe one day, when Paul tired of her and her nipper, or maybe when he just wasn't looking... He glanced at Paul, making sure his sneaky leering at Mary couldn't be detected. He wanted to look more, but couldn't risk it, so he looked for opportunities to look in her direction.

"You making one of them coffees for me, Mary?" he asked, taking in her breasts, undressing her with his eyes, and imagining what it would be like to run his hands over her soft, silky skin and down to her crotch.

Mary felt the uncomfortable penetration of his eyes, but when she looked up to catch him he had averted his gaze back to Paul, as though it had been only in her imagination. Occasionally in the past she had caught his look. Their eyes had met, but when this happened it was usually Mary who blinked first, discomfited, a cold sweat on the back of her neck. Sometimes his look penetrated deep into her soul and left her feeling empty. It was as if he could see, as if he knew. As if he had been there before.

"Should be a good game, eh, Paul?" Bully asked, wishing he could have just half an hour alone with the slut. Then he'd teach her. He thought how wonderful it would be to beat up on her before having her. That would teach her for the way she looked at him.

He'd often thought about it, trying to live what it would be like in his dreams, but the frustration made him angry. He wanted the real thing and not another fantasy like all his others. And even now as he thought about it his hands were forming tight fists as if squeezing the life out of her. Maybe when Paul wasn't around he would have her. He would use her to take revenge for all the hurt heaped on him by the prostitutes he visited.

Some of the girls worked the streets for Steve Pierce. Bully loved their slutty work clothes: their short skirts riding up over their bums when leaning into a punter's car, their extra-high-heeled leather boots, the slutty, exaggerated walk, advertising their wares. Stevie Pierce owned them; he controlled them. He was their provider, nurturing them and protecting them, but if they misbehaved or wouldn't work he would have the crap beaten out of them. They feared him, but needed him, and Bully was his gofer. Sometimes, if he was lucky, one of the girls would be so desperate that when they hadn't the money for a fix they would give him satisfaction for free – usually a hand job. And sometimes he could take advantage of them when they were drugged out of their skulls, but only sometimes, and only a grope. "Don't mess with the merchandise," Steve Pierce would say, but then, what did he know? Stevie Pierce wasn't interested in the merchandise. His interest was boys.

Mary was different; she was out of reach. He couldn't get to her, at least not while Paul was around. She was a slut, a prize to be taken, but she wasn't a druggy and she wasn't a whore. She wasn't desperate, She didn't belong to Stevie Pierce, and he couldn't have her. She drove him mad… *Mary, Mary, quite contrary, how does your garden grow?* Bully sipped the mug of coffee she gave him, his fist tightening on the handle.

Chapter Seven: Charlie

They played dominoes down the Nag's Head, Shaker, Mary and Paul, Mary slowly sipping her glass of beer shandy, making it last. Paul tapped the table with a domino. *Shit*, he thought, taking a long swig emptying his glass. *I can't do anything with these pieces.* He was bored with dominoes, his interest lasting only as long as he was winning, which he wasn't. He had lost the last three games hopelessly. Shaker always played a strategic game, closing it down and making it difficult for Paul to play. He was a bastard, that Shaker, a fucking bastard, and if his head ever stopped shaking, Paul would knock it off. That would stop the fucker shaking!

"Shaker, you're a fucking jammy bastard!" Paul exclaimed, grinning. "You got any money, Shaker? It's time for another pint!"

Shaker shook his head, or at least that was what Paul thought he had done. They were both broke.

Paul looked at Mary hopefully. "Lend us a fiver, Mary."

"I ain't got none!" Mary grabbed her purse from the table and held it tight in case Paul reached for it.

"Fuck me, Mary, didn't you get your child's allowance from the social?"

"Yeah, but I'm spending that on Michelle."

"You fucking spoil that kid!"

"She needs a new pair of shoes!"

Paul gave up. There was no dealing with Mary when she was in that mood. He thought instead of how he really hated the smell of pubs and stale beer. He remembered the stench of his dad's foul breath, the spit as he pulled his face close, and the hardness of his fist. He remembered the seemingly endless hours in the evening waiting outside in the cold whilst his mum and dad drank ale in the bar, and the sound of music and laughter from the mysterious world within as the door with its ornate window swung open, belching out the smell of stale smoke and beer. He remembered too the jolly cockle-man with cockles in vinegar in tubs. His mum would bring him a bag of crisps and a glass of lemonade. "Here you are, son!" she would say. "We won't be long now."

But they would always be long, from opening to closing time, when he would hear the bell and the call of "Time, gentlemen, please!", and then it would be another hour before they staggered out into the cold. His mum would ruffle his hair and he would try to smile as though he had been enjoying himself, and they would walk home.

Often he would fall behind as his mum and dad argued, arguing about nothing at all. They were always at it. There was no beginning and no end, a continual round of pulling one way or another, his dad's voice louder and louder, booming, as they started shouting at each other, about what Paul neither knew nor understood. He would cover his ears with his hands, but it did no good. "Don't worry, love," his mum would say as they got home. "It's just the drink talking, that's all it is!" The drink! How the fuck could drink talk?

But it wasn't long before his dad would fall asleep. The drink did that too, which was a blessing. He would fall into the armchair as soon as they got home, demand a cup of tea and before it arrived he would be asleep.

Paul used to wonder how easy it would be to take a bottle or a knife and do him in – to get rid of him forever – but he never did. What he really wanted was his dad's affection, some acknowledgement, and some respect. He wanted someone he could look up to, someone who would let him be a child.

"Look, Dad, I made a spoon for the tea caddy in metal work at school!" The metalwork teacher was Scottish and had a very thin face and pointed nose, and the classroom had a hot-metal smell about it. Paul thought that perhaps the teacher had been bashed out of a piece of metal too; warm, soft metal like gold, perhaps. He was always encouraging. "That's a good effort, son!" he had said in his Glaswegian drawl. But it didn't cut any ice with his dad.

"Don't bother me now, son. Can't you see I'm reading the paper? Show it to your ma!" his father had said.

"Ma! I made a tea caddy spoon at school. Look!"

The tea caddy spoon was put in a drawer and never used. They continued to use the silver spoon with a crown on the handle. "That was from the Queen's coronation, was that spoon. I've had it since I was a nipper," his mum had declared. No need, then, for his caddy spoon.

Uncle Charlie was different. Uncle Charlie was in the Army, and when he was on leave he would visit and stay for a few days, or a week or two. He had badges on his arms, with bright colours and a dragon. Charlie was in a Welsh regiment, which puzzled Paul because Uncle Charlie wasn't Welsh. Uncle Charlie was fun, always with a joke to break the ice-cold atmosphere of the house when Paul's dad was in a mood.

Charlie seemed to bring something out of Paul's dad. Even Paul's dad would smile at Charlie's jokes and listen to his stories. Uncle Charlie was an engineer, or some-such. Paul's dad called him 'Chalky', but Paul didn't know why. Charlie was his mum's brother, and he and his dad had been at school together.

Uncle Charlie sang with a beautiful voice like Bing Crosby. He would sing *I'm Dreaming of a White Christmas* and *Singing in the Rain*. He could play the out-of-tune piano in the pub with a kind of *thump, thump* on the bass keys and *tinkle, tinkle* with his right hand. It was as if his fingers landed haphazardly on the keys, and yet they would be the right notes.

"He took to the piano like a fish to water, did your Uncle Charlie!" Paul's mum had said. "It came quite natural. He never had no lessons, you know. Just picks it out by ear, he does."

All the numbers Charlie played had the same rhythm, or at least Paul thought so, but they were fun – *thump, thump, tinkle, tinkle, roll out the barrel, let's have a barrel of fun, tinkle, tinkle, thump, thump* – and Paul could hear it as he supped his lemonade on the bench outside. He could hear the boisterous laughter and the singing as everyone joined in a chorus or a familiar verse, and Paul's foot tapped and danced on the pavement as he wished he could go inside.

When the door opened, the music and laughter would be louder. People would be laughing, people shouting, and often someone would be telling everyone else what was what.

"There's no point in voting for any of them, I'll tell you straight. They're all in it for themselves. And if you think they care a jot for us lot, then you're sadly mistaken. Delusional." Or some such oratory.

"You're right there, Ted!"

"Give us another tune, Charlie. That'll see to it."

Uncle Charlie would bring him lemonade with a lump of ice-cream in it that made it froth and taste fantastic. Even the bag of crisps tasted better with its little blue-paper bag of salt that you shook, and then you'd suck on the salty paper. "There you are, son!" he would say as he handed Paul another glass of lemonade. He never forgot Paul; he would always look out for him. But then he would be gone and not seen for another six months or so, not until he had more leave.

Uncle Charlie was Paul's first pop idol. He would try and comb his hair in the same style, except Uncle Charlie's hair was short and looked as though it had been cut with a basin on his head – 'short back and sides', he called it, and it was Army regulation. Uncle Charlie always had the scent of hair gel and aftershave, and he was always well manicured. His boots would shine so that you could see your face in them – 'spit and polish', he called it – and his boots creaked and squeaked when he walked. His trousers were always neatly pressed, and his tie immaculately knotted. He wore gold cufflinks and shirts with starched, stiff, detachable collars. He told Paul's mum that he spent most of his time 'square-bashing', and Paul had wondered what that was: what kind of squares needed bashing and why it was a job for the Army.

Charlie fished. He would set off on the train into the countryside somewhere, to a lake or river, cast his line, and sit quietly for hours, occasionally recasting his line with its hook and maggot on the end. Paul couldn't recall him ever catching anything, or if he did he never brought it home. Occasionally, Paul went with him and sat silently so as not to 'disturb the fish'. Silently they sat, waiting. Charlie would say very little, but he would look thoughtful, so Paul would look equally thoughtful. And after two hours of looking thoughtful, Charlie would speak.

"What do you say about a cup of tea, lad?" A very profound suggestion, Paul thought, as Charlie would open a basket with neatly packed cheese and ham sandwiches and a thermos flask of tea. The way Charlie took out the contents of the basket was as methodical as the way he had placed them in it. Each was carefully placed to fit neatly, and with military precision, and Paul would imagine they were on a secret mission. Catching fish was simply a cover, he thought, else it was madness to sit for hours for little or no reward but for the occasional excitement of a poor fish taking a bite from the hook.

Paul came to the conclusion that Charlie didn't really want to catch the fish – a nibble would do, if only to confirm that there were still fish to be had. Paul once asked him if he had caught anything, ever.

"It's all about the doing, not the taking, lad," Charlie had replied, philosophically. "If you do things right, good will come of it," he often said. "No point in achieving something if you do it wrong."

So, fishing with Charlie wasn't about catching fish. Paul never discovered exactly what it *was* about, although Charlie told him it had a lot to do with 'patience'.

"Are we going to catch any fish, Uncle Charlie?" Paul would ask.

"Patience, lad, that's the thing. You've got to be patient."

There seemed to be no limit to patience. Uncle Charlie, Paul concluded, would be happy with lots of patience and no fish.

Charlie would often tell stories that had a lot to do with patience, Paul recalled. Once, when they were fishing, he told Paul a story of a boy who couldn't resist a plum. It was the last plum in a bowl on a table, and the boy took it and gobbled it down, but the plum had a grub in it and the grub had made the boy very ill with a bad tummy-ache.

"Now, lad, what does that tell you?" Charlie had asked.

"Not to be greedy?" Paul had suggested.

"Ah, yes, but you see, lad, it tells you more than that!" Charlie declared. "It teaches a lot, does that tale, lad."

Paul looked puzzled, but Charlie explained. "Number one," Charlie continued. "Always ask why something has been left. Why was it the remaining plum?" It wasn't just that the boy had been greedy. He may not have been greedy at all, and it might have been the only plum he had. There was nothing in the story that would say the boy was greedy. No, it wasn't greed. It was haste: acting without thinking was his downfall. Haste, and the lack of consideration of the possibilities.

He was full of wisdom, was Charlie, Paul thought.

Each morning, Charlie would polish his shoes or boots, all of them, lining them up at the foot of his bed. He would use a bit of spit along with the polish, which he applied with a spoon, methodically working it into the leather. Paul was taken by how much effort Charlie would put into it. It was like a ritual, he thought. Paul also noticed how everything would be neatly arranged in his haversack or in his suitcase.

"Everything has its place, lad," he had explained when Paul asked him about it. "Everywhere there is structure, order, and rhythm." And then he had said something profound – at least, Paul thought it was profound. It sounded profound, although Paul didn't really understand it: "A tangled knot is no good to anyone, Paul."

A tangled knot... Paul often considered what his Uncle Charlie had meant by it. Sometimes, Paul thought, life was like that too: a tangled knot that you couldn't undo easily.

Chapter Eight: On Gossamer Wings

Uncle Charlie killed a man and went to prison for it. Manslaughter, they called it. Gentle Charlie got into a fight in a seedy downtown bar near an Army base in Germany. He stepped in, trying to stop trouble, he said. His mate was in danger, threatened by a knife, and Charlie acted instinctively. The next he knew, the big German man was on the floor with his head smashed and seeping blood. They said he'd bashed it on the edge of a table as he fell. Charlie had knocked him down with one penetrating punch to the side his head. Staggering sideways, the man's legs gave way and he crashed to the stone floor.

It wasn't the only brawl Charlie had ever been involved in, but he had an exemplary Army record, they said. He was a good soldier, but an example had to be set and there was the question of diplomatic relations. This kind of thing had to be stamped out. So an innocent man, Charlie, went to prison for it, prematurely ending his Army career. He was a broken man.

Charlie served just two years in prison, although for him it seemed like an age, and when he was out he returned to England. He stayed at first with Paul's mum and dad, but it didn't work and it wasn't long before they were falling out. Charlie had changed, and Paul mostly now kept out of his way. He would run home as fast as possible from school looking forward to seeing his uncle, but his mum would warn him to be quiet and go out and play. Charlie spent most of his time sleeping or just sitting in a chair staring at the wall.

"What's up with Uncle Charlie?" Paul would ask, but his mum wouldn't tell him. His mum couldn't tell him, as she didn't know, although she tried hard to be understanding.

"Don't bother me now!" he would say. It was as if someone had died in the house, and in a way someone had: Uncle Charlie. Or at least, a dead man had come to stay. Paul began to think that Charlie wasn't his uncle at all, that he was just a man who resembled Charlie and who had come to stay by mistake. Disappointed and hurt, he began to hate him, and kept out of his way.

A few months after he had come to stay, Charlie left and Paul didn't see him again for what seemed like years. Then he learned that Charlie was back in prison. He had hit a man, his mum said, and that is all she would say. "Best place for him!" his father would say. "At least he isn't living rough like a tramp!"

***

Annie watched Charlie shuffling from bin to bin, sifting through the empty and half-empty soggy cartons or bags of this or that, searching diligently for a morsel of food – a leftover from a discarded fish and chip supper or a half-eaten burger – his dirty fingers dipping deep into each bin, pulling the paper wrappers aside, tearing into this and that: a rain-sodden box with a half-eaten fried chicken leg.

Sometimes he would sit silently on the bench and Annie would sit next to him. She knew Charlie. She had known Charlie all those years ago when they were kids, but now he was barely recognisable. Even his own family wouldn't know him – the family that had disowned him years before or had just simply forgotten he was there, somewhere – abroad, in prison, drunk, lost – until finally he barely struck their imagination. He was just a distant conscience. They passed him in the street without recognition; they crossed the road in case he smelled, which often he did. Charlie stank, and the only people who didn't notice were the growing band of other stinkers, the lost souls hiding from this or that as they gathered for warmth in this drop-out centre here or there, or under the bridge. Once, the children gave him a bottle of milk. Smiling through his unkempt beard, he bent down to take it from them with his weather-beaten, dirty fingers, and with the other hand he touched a child's nose. Screeching, they ran off, half fearful, adrenalin pumping, excited, a dare fulfilled.

Often he would hear Annie's voice in his head, almost as though she was there beside him. It was a voice like all the other voices in his head, some tormenting, some sweet like Annie's – harsh voices, demanding voices, haunting voices, lost voices, voices past, forever past.

He didn't speak. He had nothing to say. Sometimes he would feel his long fingers on the ebony and ivory – *'roll out the barrel'* – and he would mutter the words.

Lost in his straggly unkempt, brown-greying beard, he would tap with his foot, and he could smell again the sweet taste of beer, see the laughing faces. "Give us another, Charlie!" they would cry as one or other placed another full tankard on the worn piano top. "Give us another, Charlie!" It was an echo in a distant memory.

"If you were the only girl in the world, and I was the only boy. Nothing else would matter...in... the ...world..." Charlie's fingers slowed and stopped playing, a tear in his eye, his throat choked, the imaginary piano dissolving.

"Nothing else would matter in the world today. We would go on loving in the same old way," Annie's voice, sweet, soft, almost a whisper, sweetly singing. "Go on, Charlie! *A garden of Eden just made for two, with nothing to mar our joy.* Dad used to sing that song, Charlie."

"Goes a long way back, Annie. It goes a long way back."

Charlie had a sweet, mellow voice, and when he sang, he and Annie were transported to another time, another place: *"Fly me to the moon and let me swing among the stars"; "It was just one of those things, just one of those nights, just one of those fabulous flights, a trip to the moon on gossamer wings..."* Charlie liked the line about 'gossamer wings'; Annie liked the 'trip to the moon'. They liked the oldies the best. Annie loved a song that had a line about the moon being made of paper, but she couldn't remember what it was. *"It's only a paper moon,"* Charlie had remembered.

They were such lovely songs, songs that brought tears to Charlie's eyes, and he would look into a far distance, a void, and nothing was there – an absence, an ache.

"But it wouldn't be make-believe if you believe in me," Annie sang, prompting, bringing him back.

"Oh Annie, Annie, it's been such a long time, Annie."

"I know, Charlie, I know. Such a long time!"

Annie felt Charlie's pain, the aching in his heart – the lost love, the forever love, the undying, blue, purple love. Charlie was full of love – a giving, not a taking love. It was, Annie felt, as though his heart reached out, embracing the world. Charlie had no knowledge of hate, bitterness, envy or greed. He knew not whether he had abandoned the world, or they him. He loved the scent of the flowers, and the damp sweet smell of the dew.

He would dance with Annie in the moonlight, and Annie would grow old. They would be together, Annie and he, as it would have been, as it should have been. They would be married and come and sit beneath the moon, on this, their bench, and there would be their initials carved along with the others: *C loves A.*

"I love you, Charlie!"

"I love you too, Annie!"

Annie felt the life betrayed, taken – a history that would have been, a possible, a not. A voice in his head, along with all the other voices.

Chapter Nine: Kate

Her heels carved two lines in the semi-hard crust of earth. One shoe had been pulled off as Kate's body was dragged, slowly, a metre or so at a time, deeper into the bushes lining the stream leading to the lake. She was heavier than he had thought now that she was dead. Her head lolled back, and her swollen, bruised and bloodied lips seemed to sneer at him even in death. He let her drop to the ground.

"Fucking bitch!"

It was bitterly cold. He breathed into his cupped hands to warm them. His hands were cold, but his body was warm and sweaty. He grabbed again beneath her arms, pulling her up and tugging her body another two metres to the ditch. Her firm, young, naked breasts made him want her again, but it was too late. She was dead – a piece of meat, another whore taken from this miserable world.

She shouldn't have laughed at him; she shouldn't have mocked him. If she had just given him what he wanted then she wouldn't be dead, and he would be enjoying her body again. She was like the others: a fucking whore who needed to be taught a lesson. Her neck had snapped so easily, and then he had raped her warm but lifeless body – the body he now watched with delight as it rolled down into the ditch, lifeless arms and legs folding like a rubber doll's. He felt the scratch on his cheek. The bitch had scratched him!

That night it snowed heavily, and it snowed the next night and the next, steadily through the days and nights with brief periods of cloudless sky – a cold blue sky, freezing her body, covering it, hiding it just as it was also hidden from view by the shrubs lining the ditch and the path.

It was the cruellest of winters. The snow lay thick on the ground for weeks, and in some places it was knee-deep. The trains stopped, the buses stopped; the world stopped. When there wasn't a blizzard, children came wrapped up in coats, mittens and scarves; they threw snowballs and made snowmen. For most of them, the lake was out of bounds, difficult to reach because of the thick snow and harbouring danger where the ice might break on the thick, frozen surface of the lake.

Annie knew what it was like to be missing, and now Kate was missing. It took several days before it was noticed she was gone, and another few weeks for her acquaintances to realise she was unlikely to return.

It was the punters who missed her first, the regulars who had now to make do with one of the other girls. "What happened to Kate?"; "Where's Mandy? Have you seen her about?"; "Where's Shirley?", they would ask with just a passing interest. Many didn't even know her name, using just any name, or any of the other street names she used: Sasha, Natasha, Yvonne… It only made a difference, if it made any difference at all, in that they had to ask for what they wanted, to go through the embarrassment of asking, where Kate knew and always pleased her regulars: a blow job was a blow job no matter which girl gave it, and some could talk dirty better than Kate.

For only the kinkiest did it really matter that much. And then there was a new girl on the block, occupying the same spot Kate had used. Nature abhors a vacuum, and soon it was filled.

The girls thought Kate had gone to stay with her sick mum, who hadn't seen her for much of the year. So no one really missed her. She was gone, not missing. She could have been gone for years and still not be missed, but Annie knew she was missing. She wasn't the first, and she probably wouldn't be the last.

***

"They still haven't done nothing about it!" Mary declared, looking out at the snow-covered landscape.

Paul, shaking the newspaper as if to say 'shut up, girl, can't you see I'm reading?', muttered something inaudible.

"Mum hasn't been able to get here for days now, that hill is so slippery!"

"They don't care shit, girl! We ain't their priority, see!"

"They gritted the road, but did nothing about the pavement!"

"Fuckwits!"

She could see Bully Spence slipping and sliding up the hill.

"Are you expecting Bully Spence?"

"No. Why?"

"He's coming up the hill."

"Shit!"

Mary wondered what they were up to. She didn't believe Paul wasn't expecting him.

"Put the kettle on, love. He will be here soon."

"Since when have we put ourselves out to make tea for that toe-rag?"

"Don't argue girl, just do it, OK? We've got some things to sort out, that's all."

Things to sort out, as if that was sufficient explanation, Mary thought. What kind of things, she dared not ask.

***

Mary could still see the scar on Bully Spence's cheek – a thin, white line. She had noticed it weeks before when it was still red. She would have liked to scratch his face too, the oily fat pig. He'd said he'd scratched it on a piece of wire dangling from a fence, and Paul said that was most likely. But what he had really been doing, Mary couldn't think.

Bully slurped his tea, holding the cup so that it didn't tilt as he brought it to his lips. Mary noticed his hands were shaking.

"I just need to get away for a while," he was explaining to Paul.

Paul had mentioned to Mary that he thought Bully had crossed with Steve Pierce. Nobody crossed with Pierce and got away lightly.

"It'll blow over," Paul said, with little reassurance. "It's not your fault the silly cow ran off!"

Mary asked what they were talking about, but she knew that was never a good thing to do. And she knew already, of course.

One of Pierce's girls had disappeared and hadn't been seen on the streets for weeks. Pierce didn't like his girls not working; they had to be kept in check. Bully was supposed to keep an eye on them and keep them in order, and if one was playing up then Bully was first in line to take action.

Pierce's girls... how easy it would have been to become one, Mary thought. She knew at least two of the younger ones. She had known them since they were children together. *Children together...* how long ago that seemed for such a short time to have passed. Were all of Pierce's girls 'legal'? Mary doubted it. She wished that Paul was not involved with Pierce.

But not only had one of his girls gone missing, the police had become involved, and that too would not please Stevie Pierce.

"If we don't trouble them," he had told Bully, time and again, "then they won't trouble us." But now the police *were* troubled, and Stevie Pierce was troubled. So now the estate had also been troubled.

Flashing blue lights always meant trouble, and for two nights in a row the estate had been a blaze of blue, flashing like a niggling toothache.

It wasn't that uncommon, the occasional slow drive-through, the screeching brakes, sirens blaring, blue lights flashing, the chase of a stolen car, a vehicle used in a robbery, a vehicle stolen for a joyride or a lad running and being chased. That might be daily. But this was a different presence: several police vehicles were parked almost at random, and dozens of police officers prowled the estate, talking to the girls on Needle Alley. That was more unusual, and for most it was an unpleasant infestation, a time to go underground and not be seen. A deathly hush descended on the 'usual' business of the estate: deals here, deals there, items changing hands with nods and winks. Now all was quiet, waiting for whatever it was to blow over.

Chapter Ten: Charlie's 'It'

This was Annie's world: rows and rows of houses with chimneys smoking silently, softly; rows and rows of doors with polished brass knockers, and grey stone doorsteps, scrubbed; steps to the pavement with no front garden; rows and rows of back-to-back houses – street after street where mums cooked and darned, knitted and scrubbed.

Out in the streets, children played in little groups, and in the mornings they would come out of their doors and parade down to the infants' or junior school. The siren sang for the factory towering over the small town, and the school bell rang for the children, Everything had its place, its time, and its purpose, and they would all go to chapel or church on Sunday in their neatly pressed clothes.

There was Johnnie with a runny nose, a nose that always ran, but he always had his cap on. There was 'ginger' Thomas, with his freckles and his mischievous smile, and there was Simon whose dad drank home-brewed beer and recited the works of Shakespeare. There was Barry, always pushing and shoving and wrestling, and Frank who dribbled a ball. Endlessly he'd pick it up and put it down, bouncing from one knee to the other – once, twice, thrice, and then he'd balance it on his foot, kicking it against the end terrace wall – the wall where they chalked the stumps for cricket, and where they hit the old, dirty tennis ball back and forth. There they were with their shirts hanging out and their shoes scuffed. There they were, down at the brook with their feet wet, looking for 'tiddlers' with jam jars with makeshift string handles. There they were when time went slowly, each day an age, where they would fight the battles of World War Two, five years in a day, and where they would hop and skip, riding ghostly horses. There they were with their scuffed knees; there they were in innocence with bread and jam for tea.

There they were, Annie and Charlie, Charlie with a conker on a string – a champion conker soaked in vinegar to make it hard. There was Charlie with his wine gums: chewy, firm and full of fruity mouth-watering flavour. There was Charlie with his multicoloured marbles. And there was Rose.

There was Rose, hopping and skipping, playing hop-scotch. There they were, Annie and Rose. Round and round the tree they ran, and up and down the street. And there was Cedric, Rose's brother. Round and round the tree they ran, and up and down the street. There was Charlie; there was Rose; there was Cedric.

"You're 'it', Charlie!"

Charlie covered his eyes. Charlie was always 'it'. The others ran and hid.

"One, two, three, four, five!" Charlie counted slowly, clearly, out loud, and reaching twenty the air rang with his melodramatic voice, "I'm coming to get you!"

Annie loved the thrill, waiting until the count reached eighteen before finally deciding to hide here or there – a last-second dash, ducking, diving, and holding her breath. Once she hid in a rubbish bin.

Nobody found her, and she gave herself away by lifting the lid.

Cedric was the worst, because he always made such noise. Nobody breathed as heavily as Cedric. Cedric clumped with his feet; Cedric banged doors. But Annie was fast and silent, and she could hold her breath longer than the others. She could roll up into a ball and stay ever so quiet, blending stealthily, like a cat in the undergrowth. She could climb up or crawl under. She could take up a position like the branch of a tree and stay ever so still. They would walk around her without seeing; they would peer in but not see her, hidden in the darkness. Sometimes, when they played chase, she would run off down the path to the brook and disappear into nowhere as they followed behind. One moment she was there, the next she had gone, and they would spend ages trying to find her. Annie was magic.

***

"You're 'it', Charlie!" Annie cried. But Charlie couldn't hear as he rummaged through the litter. It wasn't that Charlie didn't talk to Annie; Annie heard all that Charlie said. But Charlie heard only a fleeting echo, mixed with the jumble of words in his head and the voices he heard.

"You're 'it', Charlie!"

"Oh, Annie! Is that you?" But Annie came and went; a whisper; a wisp hiding in his head.

Sometimes he would try to shake his head clear, but the voices wouldn't let go – louder and louder, banging and banging, until his head burst and he would scream. He would never be free, but sometimes Annie would soothe him. Sometimes she managed this.

"It's OK, Charlie. It's OK," her voice would say.

"Come on, pretty baby. Let's a move it and a-groove it."

"Shake it, baby, shake it. Honey, please don't lose it."

Move It by Cliff Richard and the Shadows – the first record Charlie had owned. His mum had bought it for him. He'd taken it in to school and they'd all listened to it on the record player in the classroom, the one they used to play country dances, when they'd all take partners and twirl around in time to the music. Mrs Welsh seemed to like it too. Charlie liked Mrs Welsh. Charlie liked Annie too, and Annie loved *Move It*.

"Charlie, you're an angel!" she cried. "Look, Rose. Charlie's got *Move It*."

And Charlie swelled; he stood tall because Annie liked *Move It*. They danced, and Mrs Welsh danced too.

"You're 'it', Charlie!"

"One, two, three, four, five… sixteen, seventeen, eighteen…" And Annie hid, but they never found her and they never saw her again.

Chapter Eleven: And Snow Lay All Around

"I think she's sleeping," Mary said, holding back the tears, as she and Paul came to the hospital bed. "Hello, Mum!"

But Mum didn't answer. Mary looked anxiously at the nurse, who had already told her that it was 'touch and go', and the doctor had said that if she did make a recovery it was difficult to predict the outcome. "We shall have to wait and see. Only time will tell!" he had said gravely, almost in a whisper.

Mary's mum was very poorly. It had been three hours since they brought her in after she had collapsed while drinking a cup of tea. They had to get an ambulance to take her. A mini-stroke, they thought it was, but it turned out there was little that was 'mini' about it. One minute she had been talking, then one side of her face looked funny and droopy. Mary held her hand now as she had in the ambulance – a hand worn by the years caring for others and with the ring her father had given her on their wedding day.

They'd had to carry her down the stairs because the lift wasn't working. She had looked so frightened, so scared, her eyes like those of a child looking for comfort, looking for any sign that all would be well. But Mary was scared too, even as she tried to be strong. "You'll be all right, Mum. The ambulance is here!" But she wasn't alright; she was very poorly.

Rose was Mary's rock and now she was crumbling. "Please, Lord," Mary pleaded silently, "don't take her away!"

The doctors said she was 'stable' but they were concerned and thought it unlikely she would pull through. Rose thought she would die, and Mary thought her mum would die. Mary leaned forward to hear Rose murmur.

"Annie."

"What, Mum?"

"Annie!"

"She keeps saying 'Annie'."

"Who the hell is Annie?" Paul asked. "She sounds a bit gone to me, Mary."

"No, Annie was her friend when she was little. She went missing and was never found. Mum often told me about it." Often, repeatedly, forever – it was as if Mary had grown up with Annie – invisible Annie, magic Annie, who had wings and who could fly like Mary could in her dreams.

"Ask Charlie!" Rose insisted. She didn't know how to say it, how to explain.

"Ask who, Mum? Ask what?"

"You must ask him. It needs to be put right."

"I don't understand, Mum. Who is Charlie?

But Rose slept, so tired from the burden of years, a long day finally drawing to a close. And Mary watched each breath anxiously, to be sure the Lord had not taken away.

***

"*Michelle, ma belle, sont les mots qui… la la la de da de dum…*These are words that go together well, my Michelle. That was Mum's favourite song!" Mary listened to the Beatles' refrain on the radio in the kitchen, humming along as best she could. "It was Mum who suggested we call Michelle Michelle."

Mary was like her mum, always singing along with tunes on the radio. It was a habit that irritated Paul. *"La de da dum de da la de dum"* – endless, tuneless *'dum de dahing'*, with occasional words thrown in, usually at the beginning or end of a verse. Often a whole phrase was out of time with the music, and usually sung while ironing. Mary was always ironing: ironing while making tea, watching telly, folding neatly and making piles, making balls of pairs of socks. Where the fuck did all the socks go? Mary took them down to the launderette as pairs and came back with not a single one of the same colour or size! Not that it really mattered; Paul was happy to wear the same pair for a week.

Paul grunted, before slurping his coffee, briefly interrupting the delicate art of rolling a joint.
"That's French, that song." Or at least it sounded as though that was what he said. Whatever it was he had said, Mary chose to ignore it.

"We were both listening to the radio and it was playing. John Lennon was her favourite Beatle. She told me. And I thought it was such a nice name, Michelle."

"It sounds like he sings through a fucking drainpipe!" Paul looked at his newly rolled joint, pleased with himself for his put-down and for his joint, which he held out to admire, a long, shaggy smoke.

"Who does?" Mary asked, a little confused if not surprised by Paul's description.

"Who does what?" Paul asked back, pleased that he had her attention, and still savouring his comment.

"Sings through a drainpipe."

"Fucking Paul McCartney!" Paul lit his joint, flicking the lighter several times before it would work. The flame ran up the paper like a fuse before settling down, glowing bright red when he drew on it, taking the smoke deep into his lungs and slowly blowing it out.

"Isn't it John Lennon that sings it, then?" Mary asked.

"Sings what?"

"The song... *Michelle*."

"How the fuck should I know?"

"Well, anyway, John Lennon was her favourite." After all, she thought, which Beatle had sung it wasn't the point. Mary wondered how a drainpipe might sound if it could sing. All clogged up with stuff, perhaps. Tea leaves, mostly, and fat.

Anyway, of course Paul knew that Michelle had been called Michelle from the Beatles' song. He had been there when they chose it. He had been there when Michelle was born. He had been there for Mary at the hospital.

Mary had worried about telling Paul she was pregnant. How would she tell him? When would she tell him?

"Well, Mary love, he's going to find out sooner or later," her mum had said. "It's not as if it don't show."

"But what can I say, Mum?" How could she explain, and how would Paul react? He had said nothing, but her mum was right. It wasn't that it didn't show.

"Tell him what happened, love. That's the best," her mum advised, and Mary thought her mum was always full of wisdom.

Mary didn't want to lose Paul. He had been so good to her since they had started dating. Slowly she had allowed him to touch her, to put his arms round her and then to kiss her – a deep, lovely kiss all the better for the waiting. He was so gentle for someone so rough. He was so tightly sprung, yet so gentle.

"Paul, there's something you should know. I don't really know how to tell you this, but..." she had started awkwardly. "But..." She paused briefly to consider what words to use.

"You're pregnant, girl," Paul had said, factually and unaffectedly, between licking along the rim of a cigarette paper and sticking it down by rubbing his finger along the length of it. It was a gesture that emphasised the obviousness of what he had said, as if it had been as inconsequential and as simple as rolling a cigarette.

"What?" Mary was thrown by his response. Well, it wasn't a response. It was a statement of the obvious.

"You're pregnant," he had repeated matter-of-factly. "It's fucking obvious, girl."

"But..." Mary started to cry uncontrollably. "I'm sorry, Paul. I don't know who the father is. I was raped, Paul."

Paul took her into his arms and they hugged for simply ages. "It's OK, girl. It's OK. It's not your fault."

But she still thought it was.

She looked out of the window now at the sun-bathed, shining snow melting on the ground leaving slushy patches and treacherous slippery bits. The park was clothed still in a sheet of white – smooth, an endless sea of snow, a white eiderdown covering the land; and a blanket of snow hiding the stark contrast of the ugly estate and the beauty of the park. It unified the town where once there had been a sharp divide: rich or poor, uptown, downtown, them and us. Once, on the television, she heard the estate described as a 'sink estate'. Paul had described it as 'a fucking sewer' rather than a sink, but she had thought at the time how apt it was, that sinking feeling. Here, people sank. It was where they put the 'problem families', the young single parents, the dross and the flotsam and jetsam, the 'have been', the 'never were' and 'never will be'. Here, they lived 'off the social' and never worked, masters of the art of making a bit here or a bit there.

The town had become a ghost town when the factory closed. As a child, Mary imagined the men marching and picketing the gates fighting for this or that – she never really knew what it was about – and it seemed odd to her now that they were 'fighting for their jobs' when the strike itself stopped the factory working. It was all on the telly, her mum said: the scuffles with the police, the chanting 'scab! scab!' at those who broke the strike at the factory gates, and the men joined the army of the long-term unemployed. She remembered the brass band, the banners and the men marching to the factory, back to work. The strike had failed; the men had gone back to work without winning any of their demands and within months the factory had closed and the brass band had gone with it. Her dad had gone too, and he came to her now more clearly: 'We've got to put up a fight, Ma!' he had said, but he already looked ill, his face drained and yellow with jaundice, a skull with sunken eyes, his body a thin rake. It was his last fight, and he lost. And Mary and Rose were alone in the silence of the dark house where the clock ticked on the mantelpiece – an ornate black clock, made of slate, with a lion's head on either side. There was silence where his foot had once tapped to the rhythm of his fiddle: bowing hard, bowing soft, one two three, one two three, bouncing on the strings as he jigged a jig.

The clear blue sky and the sun belied the cold. It was cold, with an icy, chilling wind. When she had been shopping it had been almost impossible to get warm. The wind pulled and tugged until it found a way in, penetrating her clothing and freezing her to the marrow.

"Brrr! It's still freezing out there!" The memory chilled her, and although the flat was warm, she still felt uncomfortably cold.

"Yeah, brass monkeys!" Paul laughed. Mary wondered what was so funny about brass monkeys, or what brass monkeys had to do with it. "It's cold enough to freeze the balls off them!" Paul explained.

"Well, it's cold, anyway!" Mary looked unimpressed by the joke. Sometimes their humour found little common ground.

Chapter Twelve: Hide and Seek!

"Charlie's 'it'! Charlie's 'it'!" Annie called excitedly, and Rose ran fast to hide as Charlie started to count, slowly and rhythmically. Rose was always on the plump side, unlike Annie, who could hide her skinny frame in almost anything with a crack in it that she could slide through. Annie always hid inside this or that: the rusting corrugated iron shed that rattled in the wind, the wide pipe that led to the brook from the disused mill. She would slide her thin frame in and out, even the old tree stump with its cavernous inside, a home for wizards, witches, and elves in the night that made Rose shiver with fright. Rose always hid *behind* this or that, and often this or that was also hiding Annie. They would touch and shush each other and hold their breaths.

Through the darkness, a light. Rose reached out to it, followed it – the end of a long tunnel, a never-ending end. When she turned, Rose found only the light again in the distance – sideways, left or right, a never-ending tunnel, whichever way she looked. She saw the occasional face, a dim blur, shading in and out of focus: Mary, Paul, Annie, Charlie, Annie. Forever Annie. "Charlie's 'it', Rose! Run!" Faster she ran as Charlie counted, goose pimples on her neck, and she ran until she could hear him no more. First, the sound of Annie's breath, at her side, and then it was gone. Then there was silence, but for the sound of her own heartbeat – loud, louder, so loud, pounding in her chest as if it might explode. Then Charlie breathing at her side, panting, running.

"I can see you!" Charlie shouted. "I can see Rose!"

"Where are you, Charlie? I can't see you! Where is Annie?"

Suddenly, Charlie was at her side. "I don't know. I looked but I can't find her."

"She can't be far, Charlie! We must look again."

The day Hearnville Road School burned down, they could see the smoke and flames for miles around. Mrs Sharpe was the first to see the smoke through her kitchen window at the top of the hill. Within seconds she was rushing out into the street, wiping her hands on her apron, shouting, "Fire! The school's on fire!" and banging loudly on the neighbour's door. A few moments later, everyone was out in the street listening anxiously to the sound of the fire engine bell. The smoke now belched dark, blackening the sky, and they could see flames reaching like fingers, grasping, lapping out of the school windows. The school was engulfed in minutes as the wind whipped ferociously at the flames storming through the classrooms.

At some point the boiler exploded with a loud boom that rocked the neighbourhood. By the time the firemen had the fire under control, it was too late. The school was destroyed, a burnt-out shell of Victorian brickwork. The roof had collapsed, and the rows of little desks with their ink wells where Rose, Charlie, Annie and others had sat were piles of black ash. Only the large radiator upon which Mrs Fletcher warmed herself while she was teaching, rubbing her hands over the warm grill as she spoke to the class, survived,

- 116 -

standing sentinel against the charred wall where the map of the world had hung with its pink colours indicating the Commonwealth. When Mrs Fletcher had once asked her what she wanted to be when she grew up, Rose had replied that she wanted "to be a teacher, Miss", but she didn't say it was because she wanted to warm her hands on the radiator. The school they had walked to in the mornings in the rain or snow, sleet or sun – walking together in secretive huddles, the girls giggling, the boys pushing and shoving, in their little raincoats and with their satchels, and with their hair combed or done in braids   lay now in ruins, a burnt-out ember of a previous age. The little lockers where they hung their coats were mangled, and the assembly hall where they sat cross-legged on the floor and listened to Mr Hart telling them how fortunate they were, where they sang hymns and where they had country dancing on Thursday afternoons... all of it was gone.

It was difficult for the children to understand. They had been getting ready to go to school, eating breakfast – hot porridge with cold milk and sugar, bread and jam, cornflakes. Rose was still in her pyjamas, her tired eyes barely open as she cleaned her teeth. She heard the sound of the fire engine, and she heard her mum cry out for them to stay in doors while she went out to see what was going on. When Rose looked out of the window she could see the smoke. She dressed quickly and bounded down the stairs and into the street to join the others, who stood speechless watching the incendiary event in the distance as their school burned down. They could see the school clearly as they looked down on it from the hill, and they could hear Mrs Braithwaite saying how it was a miracle none of the children were at school – as if God had simultaneously caused the fire but saved the children. Rose wondered why God should have destroyed such a fine school, where she felt comfortable and warm and where she painted pictures that the teacher put on the wall.

The school caretaker, Mr Smailing, was the only person injured in the fire, and he was taken to hospital with burns to his hands and smoke inhalation. Rose never saw Mr Smailing again, and she often wondered what had happened to him. Perhaps he had retired early due to disability caused by the fire, been given compensation by the local authority, and moved away to somewhere by the sea.

Within a week of the fire, the children went for lessons in makeshift prefabricated cabins erected in the old school playground and in the chapel hall where Rose and her friends attended Bible classes on a Sunday. These were the three pillars of the community: the factory with its tall chimney, which Rose painted in a picture reaching to heaven, and beside it the chapel with its steeple also reaching to heaven, and somewhere above the clouds was God looking down on the school. Each had its bell or siren summoning the people to prayer. In the centre of her picture she had drawn Annie, her friend who had gone missing.

This was Rose's world, which included the tree in the school playground where she once saw the largest stag beetle with such fearsome horns that she shuddered at night thinking it might be in the room, in the dark, waiting to pounce when she was asleep. Michael Middlehurst, with his ginger hair and dishevelled grey shirt, had poked at it with a stick, and to the sound of astonished little girls' screams, it spread its wings and flew – first directly in Rose's direction. She covered her face and screamed again, before it flew off up into the tree. The thought that such a creature existed, the thought that it crawled around unseen, was bad enough, but now that she knew that it could fly it was unbearable. She wouldn't go near the tree for weeks, and she wouldn't let her mum leave the bedroom window open even the slightest. The school with its bell, the chapel with its bell, and the factory with its siren – these were constants in Rose's world. The factory was the heart of the town, with the thud, thud, and thud of its machinery sending gentle tremors through the ground, which Rose could feel sometimes with her feet on the hard kitchen floor. Early each morning the men would go to the factory. Some would walk, and Rose could hear their boots on the pavement or road, while others would cycle, each with their peaked cap and cigarette in their mouth or one kept behind an ear for later.

Chapter Thirteen: "Mary, Mary Quite Contrary"

Turning the little key, once, twice, three times, Bully listened again to the music box he held in his hand – a shiny black box with shell-shaped, mother-of-pearl inlays, while mumbling the words: *"Mary, Mary, quite contrary, how does your garden grow?"* Repeatedly he wound and rewound, opening and shutting the lid, revealing the ballerina twirling round and round. *"With silver bells and cockle shells and pretty maids all in a row."*

Several times he listened to the tune until he could bear it no longer. Clenching the twirling ballerina in his fat fist, he snapped it off. Throwing the box against the dirty light pink painted wall, it bounced back, startling the girl kneeling at his feet. Her young, firm, breasts were bared and her short skirt hitched above her waist, revealing her fancy red and black knickers, through which Bully could see the black knot of her pubic hair, and her silky smooth thighs. Landing with a thud, the box continued playing: *jingle, jingle, jingle*. Round and round the clockwork continued until it finally ran down and stopped, and while it played the girl held her skirt up so Bully could enjoy her sexy pose and decide what to do next.

"Pretty maids all in a row," he mumbled. "Pretty maids." Pretty maids like, Mary, he thought, all in a row. "One, two, three, performing just for me, you little slut."

Leaning forward, he slapped the girl's face – not too hard, but just enough to sting. *Never damage the merchandise!* he remembered. But he was thrilled by the sound of his slap, and the feel of her cheek on his hand. He was thrilled that she had to keep her skirt hitched so he could see her, watch her, possess her, and humiliate her while he slapped her. He was so thrilled that he slapped her again. She would be made to perform for him, just like the ballerina and just like he wished he could do with Mary. He thought of Mary and he slapped the girl again. "Keep your skirt up and open your thighs wider!"

"You alright up there?" the prostitute's 'maid' called anxiously from the bottom of the stairs. "Are you OK, Katrina?"

"Yes, we're fine," Bully replied agitatedly, rubbing the porcelain ballerina's head between his fat finger and thumb. "I just dropped something, that's all. We're fine, aren't we, Katrina?"

Katrina didn't reply.

"Aren't we, Katrina?" he repeated menacingly through clenched teeth, snatching the young prostitute's hand and squeezing her fingers, bending them back viciously. "Tell her, you bitch!"

"Yes, yes, OK! No, don't do that, please!"

"Tell her, you bitch, or I'll break your fingers!"

"It's OK, June!" the girl called out. "It's OK!"

Bully listened for the creaking of the loose floorboards and the volume of the television being turned up, the applause and laughter of a daytime game show audience signifying that the maid had returned to the lounge. Patience was a virtue and, once he was sure she had gone, he continued his business with the prostitute, all the while painfully bending back the fingers of her delicate hand, reminding her to keep quiet.

"You see, Mr Pierce thinks you owe him," he whispered, in case the maid was still lurking at the bottom of the stairs. It was better to be safe than sorry, and best if he wasn't interrupted. Dealing with one bitch was easier than having also to deal with the cow downstairs. The prostitute's minder was more like a man than a woman, with a square jaw and buck teeth. An ugly bitch, he thought. If he didn't know better, he would have thought she was a transvestite, which she probably was.

"Mr Pierce thinks you owe him big-time, see." Bully bent the girl's fingers back a bit more.

"No, I don't, Bully. Honest," the poor girl replied, pleading with him.

"He thinks you been taking a bit on the side, see? A bit here, a bit there." Bully continued, ignoring the pleading, and excited now by the panic in the girl's voice and in her big brown eyes. Oh, he was going to enjoy this, he thought. This one he'd take his time over. This one would learn to show him respect. Slowly, methodically, he would teach her.

"I haven't, Bully, honest. You can ask June. She'll tell you."

"You think I'd trust that ugly bitch?"

He leaned forward and fondled her breast, rubbing his fingers over her tight pink nipples. They were small but firm, just how he liked them. Pinching them hard now between his fingers and thumb, twisting them painfully, he looked into her eyes to see the effect. "He says you owe him at least a grand."

"But I don't, honest I don't."

"But he says you do, and I can only go by that. Keep your skirt up, bitch!"

"But I don't, I told you. I only just started recently. This is my first house."

Pulling a flick knife from his pocket and releasing its thin stiletto blade. Like a conjurer pulling a trick, it appeared to come from nowhere. He grabbed the girl's hair, pulling her face close to his – so close that she could feel his breath on her thick, sulky, ruby-red, lip-glossed lips, and he could smell the minty taste of the chewing gum she'd been chewing. He took a moment to breathe it in, to taste her, planning methodically what he was going to do with her. "If you say that once more, bitch, I'm going to cut this pretty baby-doll face of yours. Do you understand?"

She nodded.

First he'd have her service him in the chair, he thought, looking round the drab, darkened bedroom of the small maisonette – one of several used as a whorehouse on the estate. The curtains were closed, shutting out the light of the day. A small table lamp with a low-watt bulb gave a pale yellow light at the side of a double bed with a dirty pink eiderdown – the bed on which the bitch lay back while her clients took their thirty quid's worth. A blow job for twenty, a bit of kinky for fifty, without a rubber for sixty, and the tissue and rubber if used would be thrown in the dirty plastic bin at the side. The adverts, he knew, said 'Katrina, buxom tall blonde bitch, all services,' but this bitch was a slender, short brunette. It wouldn't matter once the clients arrived; they'd take her without noticing.

She'd just taken over as 'Katrina'. She was young, very young, and using that to advantage, Pierce would soon change the advertisement to 'Young teenage brunette' and 'Barely legal brunette with 'O' and 'A' levels'. Pierce didn't miss a trick; he knew that 'young' merchandise would always sell. "The older ones give great kinky," he once told Bully. "They're harder, and more experienced at the discipline stuff. But there are many clients who want young, Bully-boy. Very young, if you know what I mean." He touched his nose with his audaciously gold ring-laden finger. "So if they can pass as that and still be legal, then even better."

Hanging on the wardrobe door was the school uniform: blazer, Cambridge blue, white shirt and tie, a short grey skirt and a straw hat. Next time he would have the bitch wear it with short black or blue-and-white striped socks, and she could put her hair in braids. But now he'd use her as she was.

"You don't say another word, see?" Bully continued, tickling her cheek with the blade, and licking her lips with his tongue. "All you have to do is say 'yes, sir' or 'no, sir' and do as you're told, understand?"

She nodded. He pulled her hair viciously, bending her head back until she got the message. "You understand?" he repeated.

"Yes."

"Yes, what?"

"Yes, sir."

"Again!" he tugged on her hair even harder.

"Yes, sir."

"See, this is how it runs, bitch: if you give me pleasure, do what I want you to without question – and I mean really give me pleasure – then I might consider trying to straighten it out for you with Mr Pierce, see?"

Bully paused to think. To take more pleasure from her, he felt the urge to cut her, to hurt her just a bit – a tiny snitch perhaps – but he resisted. Another time, maybe, but not now. *Don't mess this up now, stay in control, stay calm.* He took a few deep breaths.

Feeling the tension and sensing his frustration, the girl froze with fear and with the uncertainty about what he would do. Sensing he was close to a boundary, she felt faint, her heart pounding, and she told herself, *Please just do it and get it over with and he'll leave.*

"See, if you do as you're told," his voice shook with anticipation. "I'll tell him he'd got it wrong, see. I could tell him you meant to pay him." He released her hair and sat back in the chair, unzipping his jeans. "I'll tell him it was all a mistake."

The girl sensed him relax as she complied. She wouldn't fight it; she'd do as he asked, then maybe he wouldn't harm her. Every ounce of her will to resist drained at that moment as she stepped back into childhood. "And another thing: you call me 'sir' or 'Mr Spence'. No. I tell you what: you call me 'Mr Spence, sir'." He couldn't quite make up his mind which of them gave him the most satisfaction. She felt his tension ebbing and flowing, but she also sensed him relax when she said in a childish voice, "Yes, Mr Spence, sir".

Bully knew he had nothing to clear with Mr Pierce. Pierce didn't even know he was there. All the girls took a bit here and there on the side, and Mr Pierce generally turned a blind eye as long as it wasn't too much. For Bully it was the new girls on the block, the green ones, who were easy fruit to pick. But he knew it might not be so easy with Katrina next time, because that bitch of a maid would probably put her wise. But for now, for an hour at least, he could have his way, and she could give him satisfaction.

Mary was temporarily banished from his mind, easing his pain.

Chapter Fourteen: Ask No Questions

From the kitchen window, Mary watched children playing in the school playground, running here and running there, skipping and hopping, the boys running after a football as if the ball had a life of its own, like a fox being chased. Small groups here and there played marbles or hopscotch, chatting and whispering in secretive huddles, laughing and shouting, although Mary couldn't hear them. Boys wrestling, girls playing pat-a-cake.

It seemed like yesterday – just nine short years – that in her little grey skirt and green blazer Mary had played and sung in the small primary school with its flat leaking roofs and large windows, the windows they painted at Christmas. Not so long ago that she'd played pat-a-cake.

> *"Pat-a-cake, pat-a-cake, baker's man,*
> *Bake me a cake as fast as you can,*
> *Pat it and prick it and mark it with a 'B',*
> *And put it in the oven for Baby and me."*

"For Baby and me," Mary whispered to herself, longing for the safe world of her childhood: her mum brushing her hair and squeezing her tight as she held back the tears. "It'll be alright, little one, you'll see!" her mum had said, unable to hold back her own tears. Within an hour of walking into the school on that first day, she had made friends and forgotten about the tears, even when she saw her mum watching through the railings at break time. Her mum had remained all morning, and only when Mary had looked up and saw her, laughter in her eyes, had her mum waved and left her. And so it had always seemed, so it had forever been: her mum was there with a hug when things went wrong.

When things went wrong – deeply, irretrievably wrong – yes, her mum had been there, and Mary wouldn't have been able to cope without her, but Rose's approach was to 'do and mend'. Mary would just have to cope, and that was that. It wasn't that her mum didn't feel her pain; she felt it as surely as did Mary and there had been many tears shed together. Yes, Mary could 'do and mend'. The 'do' bit was easier, the 'mend' harder; an ever-present, irremediable, suffocating anxiety, a floating uncertainty. It would grab and twist and occupy her, an indescribable blackness. Mary yearned for the child she had been, protected inside her, but the child was never too far from the surface. She wanted someone to 'kiss it better' and to take away the nagging, aching hurt in her soul. She wanted to return to the safety of the playground, to run and play, to skip joyfully and play ring-a-ring-a-roses. She wanted to look up and see her mum waiting at the school gate, and everything would be alright.

"They've removed the tree!" she exclaimed to herself rather than specifically to Paul.

"What tree?" he said, getting up and joining her at the window.

"The tree in the school playground. Look, they've removed it! It's gone! There's just a stump now!" And sure enough, Paul observed, there was a stump where the tree had been.

"I used to climb that tree when I was there!" Paul proclaimed. "Mr Bevan used to shout at us to stop and to come down. 'Get down from that tree this instant!', he'd shout." Paul reminisced, recalling now how he'd shin the short distance to the first big branch and pull himself up onto it. He couldn't remember why exactly, other than because it was there to be climbed.

"But it was such a lovely tree!" Mary recalled wistfully. She held back the tears. She wanted to cry. She wanted to be alone with the sense of loss. It was another cord severed.

"Yeah, I guess they just got fucking fed up of fucking shouting!"

"I didn't know you went there, Paul!"

"Of course I did! Where else is there to go?" And that was true enough. It was the only primary school for miles.

"Mum said it used to be called Hearnville Road School but it got burned down and then they rebuilt it and they renamed it Southmead when the estate was built!" Mary recalled.

"They've renamed every fucking thing!"

"I wonder why they did that."

"Probably because fucking Hearnville Road no longer fucking exists, girl!" Paul reasoned with a smile. "It must have been one of the roads that was here before the estate was built."

Another cord severed, Mary thought. Another irremediable loss.

"I don't remember you there, Paul."

"Well, I don't remember you either, girl. Jesus, it was a long time ago and I would have been leaving just as you was arriving, see."

"It doesn't seem such a long time ago!" And indeed it wasn't, really, Mary thought.

But of course it made sense. She rarely thought about the fact that Paul was older, and certainly not by five years, nor could she imagine Paul playing in the small playground, climbing the tree, or playing with marbles and conkers. She only knew Paul as he was now. She rarely thought of him in the past, even though she could often see the small child trying hard to escape his hard exterior. She saw his shyness, his overwhelming self-consciousness: head down, averting his eyes, and then the adjustment in his body as he pushed it back, raising his head high, and the fixed look of 'don't let them see you're scared'.

They stood now together for a while, staring out of the window at nothing in particular. Each of them was in their own reverie of past times until Paul broke the silence.

"Anyway, I thought you were going shopping, girl!"

"I am, and we'll pop in to see Mum too at the hospital, so we'll be back a bit late."

"That's OK," Paul replied, deep in thought. "I've got to go out too."

Ten minutes later he was out of the door, creating a chill in the room and leaving her still looking out of the window. She heard him curse the lift before it arrived; she heard the doors close and the hum of the lift's descent.

She saw him still adjusting his jacket as he sauntered across the road heading for the maisonettes, and she saw Bully Spence coming out of one of them to meet up with him. She didn't know if that was arranged or whether it was coincidence, but they both walked off down the hill together. She could see Bully speaking in an animated way, waving his arms about and gesticulating. Even from a distance he made her feel uncomfortable.

Mary wondered what it was that Paul got up to with Bully Spence. She always wondered, but she knew better than to ask. She knew it had something to do with Stevie Pierce, because with Bully Spence it always had to do with Stevie Pierce. Why Paul worked with them, she could never understand. One problem she did know was that there wasn't much in the way of other work to be had, and there were so many people looking for work that they only paid slave wages if you could get it. You signed on, took your dole and worked a bit on the side. It was the norm. It was, she thought, what almost everyone was doing.

Whatever Paul did do for Stevie Pierce, he got paid well for it, at least sometimes, but Mary tried not to guess what it was. It made her shudder to think, and it also made her fearful. But there was only one thing that Paul had that Stevie Pierce would need: muscle and an ability to use it, dispassionately if necessary. She kept it out of mind. What she didn't know wouldn't matter, which is why she rarely asked. Questions were out of the question. You didn't ask; nobody asked – a nod, a wink, a little here and a little there. A fiver, perhaps twenty kept a mouth shut, and nobody crossed Stevie Pierce; a slit throat kept their mouths shut for longer. It was such a different world from the cosy, innocent world of the primary school playground she now looked out on through the window. She recalled how much she enjoyed playing hop-scotch with her own little slither of blue and green stone as a marker: *hop, hop, hop, hop*.

Mary thought of the innocence of the children, some of whom had later become 'Pierce's girls'. She'd known many of them; she had played with them, laughed and giggled with them, and ran around the tree with them. They had gone to the secondary school together too, innocent, happy, and full of expectation going to the big school in their neat uniforms. But they had been 'turned' – changed, groomed and doomed – aged fourteen, fifteen, lured into the clutches of Stevie Pierce. She lost them. They became distant, and whilst she remained a child, they were plucked off the tree like cherries to be used and abused.

Sometimes, deep in her heart, Mary cried for a lost friend. She wanted to hug them, to share their pain – for pain it was. She would see the sleepless nights in their eyes, the tears shed when alone and the bruised bodies if they did not please. They were herded like cattle, pieces of meat – a hotel room here, a darkened alley there. It was a loveless life, a loveless need, a dependency as strong as any chain. They 'loved' their masters, desperate to please. They were Stevie Pierce's girls, and Stevie Pierce was detached, aloof from the merchandise, with boys to do his bidding. Boys like Bully Spence, boys like... Mary shuddered, scared of the question. Boys like Paul? Surely not Paul? Surely not Paul with his soft centre – shy Paul, innocent Paul, loving, caring, sweet-interior Paul. Please, God, make it not Paul! She cried for Paul. She cried for her lost friends. She wanted to touch their bruised and battered souls, to soothe them and make them better. She wanted to rescue them, like she did the moths trapped by the light of the lamp in the bedroom, an unfulfilled promise, taking them gently in her hand and releasing them at the window. But Pierce's allure was the stronger, a sticky mess, a honey-pot around which the bees would buzz.

It was a cry away, a scream away, from the innocent games of kiss they played at school. A girl would have a blindfold, a boy would give her a kiss, and she would say his name. Most times the kiss was a brief affair, a touch of lips. It was a bridge that spanned the changes they felt but could not understand. Mary too had played the game, but Alice, she remembered, had played it most. It was as if she could never remember the names – kiss after kiss, not a peck but deeper now. And now Alice was gone, another tragic pawn in Pierce's game, an endless game of kiss.

Chapter Fifteen: Paul Left a Note

Mary pushed the creaky door of the cabin, a wooden box with dirty windows that hadn't been cleaned in decades with peeling green paint, spiders' webs and dust. It had been where the deck chairs for the band concerts had once been stored, and where the park keepers still stored old, rarely-used or never-used rusting gardening equipment – redundant stuff that never seemed to get thrown away.

You could hire the deckchairs or sit on the grass for free, her mum had told her, and Mary thought of them all sitting in the sun with knotted handkerchiefs on their heads listening to the brass band on the bandstand, some eating ice-cream, others asleep with their heads lolling sideways, disturbed occasionally by a buzzing wasp or fly.

Situated around twenty yards from the bandstand by a large copse of trees and shrubs, the cabin was on a short path leading down to the brook. She remembered how they used to play hide and seek, sometimes hiding in the cramped space between the cabin and the trees, and how sometimes, if they were brave, they would climb over the railings that had been erected where a culvert drained into the brook, ignoring the large notice warning of danger and the spikes at the top of each railing.

She knew Paul used to play there too with his friends, as she and her friends had done and as generation after generation had done – just as her mum had done a generation before.

Occasionally the older children, the teenagers, would break into the cabin. They had done this so many times that the door no longer had a workable latch. The wood was rotten and broken where the lock used to be. Whatever had been of 'value' had long been removed.

Mary couldn't understand why Paul had asked her to meet him there. She had been to the shops with Michelle, and it was gone four by the time she had returned. Unsure when he had left it, his note read simply, *'Gone to park. Meet me at old cabin. Paul'*. At first she had ignored it. Perhaps it had been left earlier and she had been so late back that he probably wouldn't be there now anyway. She kept picking the note up, reading it again and again as though somehow an answer would reveal itself mysteriously, something she had missed. She turned it over and stared at the blankness of the paper as if it had been written in invisible ink.

"What the heck, Paul? What am I supposed to make of this?" She had spoken aloud, as if he had been there with her. The lack of reply hadn't made it any better.

Why the heck couldn't he have put a time on it, or said why and what was happening, instead of this silly cloak-and-dagger stuff? He knew how much she hated the secrecy, the ducking and diving and the Pierce stuff. It frightened her, and she could only think that this was what was behind the note. He knew also that she should be at the hospital to see her mum.

Usually he left notes to meet at the Nag's Head – simple perfunctory messages like, '*gone to pub,*' and '*back later*'. She suspected that is where he would be: at the Nag's Head with Shaker. More often than not, that was where he was, and that was surely where he would be now. Except, as she then realised, the Nag's Head wouldn't be open now. More often he never left notes at all. She was still in a mind to ignore it and wait until he came home. She had wondered what could be so urgent that she should meet him in the park. She had put the kettle on and made a cup of tea, but the note nagged. It demanded attention. She kept picking it up and rereading it. It was the strangeness of it that was intrusively compelling.

'*Meet me at the old cabin.*' Mary was puzzled. Why would he want her to meet him there? She put the note down again. It made no sense. She didn't want to go all the way there for no reason, and then there was Michelle. She would have to take her with her.

"Fucking hell, girl, I waited hours in the fucking freezing cold! Didn't you get my note?" she had imagined him saying when he got back. She imagined him now, pacing up and down, blowing into his hands to keep them warm.

It was another forty minutes before she picked Michelle up and carried her out with her pushchair. She had decided to go. Whatever it was about, it was better to be safe than sorry, and it wasn't too far. It was still light, and she would call in at the Nag's Head on the way to see if anyone had seen him. It would be opening soon. If Shaker was there, he was bound to know; he always knew what Paul was up to. Certainly more than she did.

But Shaker wasn't there, and nobody else had seen Paul or Shaker since they had been there at lunchtime.

"They didn't leave no message for me, then, or say where they were going?" she asked anxiously of Peter the barman.

"Not that I'm aware of, Mary. They had a pint and then left, love."

"If they come in, can you tell them I've gone to the park?"

"It's a bit late for walks in the park, Mary. Is anything wrong?"

"No. Just tell them."

Nothing wrong? Something was wrong, but she wasn't sure what it was.

A glance at the big clock in the pub told her it was now 6.15pm. She had delayed longer than she had thought. It would take her about twenty minutes, but if she rushed she would get to the bandstand before dark, although she noticed it was already dull. But if Paul was there it would be OK. They could walk home together. A voice told her to go home, but another urged her on: *"Fuck me, girl, I've been waiting ages! Didn't you get my note?"*

But when she'd arrived, he wasn't there. She peered through the dirty cabin windows into the dusty dimness within, furtively calling to see if Paul was there.

"Paul, are you there?" She thought she heard footsteps, someone moving, but there was no reply.

She wandered over to the bandstand and sat waiting on the wooden steps to the stage, Michelle thankfully asleep in the pushchair. After half an hour he hadn't appeared. Angrily, she decided to go home. She was angry with Paul, but also with herself for deciding to come – even more so for stupidly waiting for him when it was clear he wasn't there. It was beginning to get chilly. It was a clear, cold night, and she was now more than a little nervous. As she leaned forward to fasten the zip of Michelle's coat, she thought she heard a noise coming from the cabin: a thump, perhaps the sound of something falling over. It was already beginning to get dark as she pushed the pushchair closer to the cabin, keeping a distance at first. She recalled how odd it was when she watched films, how victims are drawn to dark places or to noises in the dark. "Why don't they simply run away?" she'd think. But now, here she was, tentatively moving toward the cabin, stopping occasionally to be sure – stopping and listening. A noise that should have said 'beware' strangely lured her towards it.

"Paul?" she called softly towards the cabin, edging closer to the door. "Paul, is that you?" She spoke softly, in almost a whisper.

She heard the thump again, clearly coming from within or behind the cabin, and now, tentatively, she pushed open the cabin door – easily done when the bolts that locked it shut were long gone.

"Paul?" Hearing a rustling noise, like a shoe scraping on the floor, Mary called tentatively into the darkness within. "Paul?"

"Paul, is that you?" A little louder now. Adjusting to the dark, she could just make out a figure in the gloomy recesses of the cabin. "Stop messing about! It isn't funny, you know. What are we doing here anyway?"

Paul's note had been simple, and it wasn't unusual for him to leave a note, even one without explanation, but she couldn't understand why Paul should want to meet in such a strange place. She thought perhaps he was in some kind of trouble. All she knew was that when she returned from shopping, she found the note and followed its instruction.

"Paul, what's wrong? Why are we meeting here?"

She began to think he was hiding, perhaps from the police or from Stevie Pierce's henchmen. She knew something had gone wrong with a job he had done with Bully Spence. They had returned agitated and had been whispering to each other, and then the police had swarmed all over the estate for a few days.

"It's not Paul, it's me!" Mary was startled by the sudden appearance of Bully Spence stepping forward out of the darkness.

"Jesus, Bully, you frightened me to death! Where's Paul and what are you doing here?"

Chapter Sixteen: Dance to Your Daddy

The sound of the clear running water of the brook seemed to grow louder as Bully and Mary stood in silence at the cabin. Bully paced up and down, smoking a cigarette – several cigarettes – which he drew on noisily, inhaling deeply and then slowly releasing the smoke in an affected, upwardly directed stream. It was now quite dark, and it was getting colder – not numbingly, but penetratingly cold. Mary started to worry about Michelle. With the sound of the brook, she thought of the clear water, the stones, gravel and mud, and the little fish that she loved to watch when she was a child and that she had shown Michelle – the little fish darting here and there, some fighting against the flow of the constant stream of water cascading over the smooth stones, driven, beating their tails to stay in one place, others resting in relatively still pools. The stream was in a constant rush, and the fish fought an endless battle against its incessant need to move on. She, Michelle and her mum had looked over the side of the little wooden ornamental bridge that crossed the water. Mary had lifted Michelle up so she could drop a leaf into the water, holding on to her tightly for fear of losing her over the edge, and they watched it pass under and out the other side of the bridge, appearing as if by magic. Michelle had gurgled with delight and pointed with the delicate fingers of her hand. Mary's mum had sung to her – *"Who shall have a fishy in a little dishy? Who shall have a fishy, when the boat comes in?"* – and Mary had bounced her up and down.

She had waited for her mum to say her dad had sung that song, but she didn't, and perhaps he hadn't. She had heard it on the radio, she thought.

"Dance to your Daddy, my little laddy,
Dance to your Daddy, my little man."

It was, Mary thought, the kind of song her dad might have sung. Michelle, of course, wasn't a 'little man', but she had loved the song and had giggled and gurgled along with it. Yet Mary didn't know who the daddy was, or for whom they would dance.

"Who shall be your daddy, my little lassie?" Mary reinvented the words now in her mind, rocking the pushchair backwards and forwards as Michelle slept peacefully, her head rolled to one side, resting on her shoulder. *"Who shall have a fishy, on a little dishy, when the boat comes in?"*

Although he had planned it up to a point, Bully Spence hadn't really thought what he would do if his trick of leaving the note worked. Here she was, Mary, responding to the note he had left.

"Mary, Mary, quite contrary, how does your garden grow?" Bully repeated the line aloud, but Mary ignored him. He would make her pay for that, he thought, somehow.

For Bully, it all came back to Mary – back to Mary because of what she was not, rather than for what she was. Mary was not one of Pierce's girls. Mary wasn't 'a slut', although Bully wished she was. Deep down, he believed she was. Deep down, he was convinced she must be. They all were, he considered. They all teased with their sexuality, and the more they didn't, the more they did. They presented a persistently nagging fever in his mind. The easier ones, those 'belonging' to Pierce, were like teasing toys, giving their punters a moment's gratification – a sordid blot on an otherwise pristine family life: half-lives, secret lives. They were bits on the side to be discarded, forgotten – objects of a transaction not recalled until the deep-seated compulsion returned. They were the touch of sordidness that their wives couldn't give, or that they would not wish their wives to give. Bully hated them all, despised them, but more than that, he loathed them, hated them because their games teased and taunted him. But Mary was different; Mary tormented him.

"Well, it's obvious Paul isn't coming!" Mary said suddenly, decisively, turning Michelle's pushchair round, ready to walk home. "And Michelle is getting cold."

"No, wait just a few more minutes," Bully suggested, trying to collect his thoughts. "He'll be here if he said he would be."

But Mary was already walking away briskly. She had decided, and that was that. It was cold, it was late, and she needed to get Michelle back. This was ridiculous; what could Paul have been thinking?

"He told me to tell you to wait," Bully pleaded.

Mary stopped, just for a few moments to think. "When exactly did you see him, Bully?"

"Earlier. He said to meet here."

"But when, Bully? What time was it when he told you, and what is it for? It doesn't make any sense. Didn't he say?" Mary started walking home again, determined this time not to be deterred. Something wasn't right about it at all, but she couldn't decide what it was. Better to be at home and wait for Paul to come back. But also she needed to get to the hospital to see her mum, and that was more important than these silly games.

"Hang on!" Bully called. "I'd best walk back with you. It's getting dark!"

Yes, Mary thought, it was getting dark, but Bully was the last person she would want to walk her home in the dark. And what she felt wasn't right about it all was Bully. His behaviour was always peculiar, she thought, but tonight, in the dark alone with him, he appeared menacingly grotesque.

Mary could feel him following behind. She couldn't decide whether to walk faster to get away from him, or slow down so he could catch up. She always felt uncomfortable with Bully Spence, but now he really was scaring her. What was he doing here, and where was Paul? No, there was something about it that she didn't feel was right. His presence was menacing. His voice sounded different, but she couldn't think exactly how or why. Perhaps it was all in her imagination. Most things seemed frightening in the dark, she thought. She told herself to stay calm, but her pulse was racing and a deep, sinking feeling disturbed her stomach. In her mind she was back in the alleyway at the pub with her attacker. She couldn't see him then, and she couldn't see him now.

"You love it, don't you?" She heard his voice in her mind. She felt his clammy breath on her face. In her half-conscious mind she could see him, but with no

face. She could never see her attacker's face, yet she felt she would know him.

Mary walked faster, struggling with Michelle in the pushchair. She wouldn't be able to get away from him, but at least she would be nearer home. She could hear his footsteps as if they echoed her own. He also now was walking faster on the path behind her. As she hurried, he hurried. The sound of their steps on the path grew louder, imposingly menacing in her mind. She was almost running; he was walking faster.

Reaching the brook, something made her stop and look round. Perhaps it was the sound. She could no longer hear his steps echoing her own. He wasn't there, or at least she couldn't see him in the dark, and then suddenly his voice.

"I can see you!" Bully's voice came out of the darkness.

Startled, Mary's heart beat faster. "Fuck off, Bully!" Mary tried to sound together, confident, not wanting him to sense her fear. But he had startled her again, and her heart was pounding her chest. She felt breathless. What made it worse was that she wasn't sure now from which direction his voice had come. *Hold yourself together!* she told herself. *It's only Bully Spence being silly.* But she still had an instinct to get away from him. Then she heard him again.

"Mary, Mary quite contrary how does your garden grow?"

Turning up the path running alongside the brook to the lake, Mary pushed Michelle as fast as she could, but within a couple of yards she came again to an abrupt stop. Peering into the dusk, she was convinced she could see the outlines of someone on the path ahead, or perhaps it was her imagination – a trick of the dark, a moonlit shadow of a bush swaying in the light breeze. The cold air penetrated her body. It was quiet apart from the odd sounds of the night: a faraway train, carrying a few passengers, rattling on the rails – *clanketty clank, clanketty clank* – the rustle of leaves, the continuous hum of traffic on a nearby motorway, occasionally penetrated by the sound of car horns, irritated drivers in an angry exchange. The silent noise of the drumbeat of life. How isolated it made her feel, distant, impersonal – other people's lives of no consequence to her own, coming and going about their business, with offices to leave, and homes at the ends of their journeys. How she wished she could be with them now. How different, now, the same sounds were at night – menacing, eerie – that were of no consequence in the day. If it was Bully ahead she wasn't sure how he could have got there. She had chosen the path because she wasn't able to push Michelle fast across the grass. Perhaps, she thought, he had cut across the grass to cut her off.

"I can see you!" Bully's voice penetrated the dark. Sinister, menacing, teasing.

The dark shape ahead of her moved, or at least it seemed to move with a step sideways. Mary wasn't sure. But then it appeared to be moving towards her, swaying from side to side.

She turned to the right, to the left. She looked backwards and then forwards again, trying to decide in which direction to run. And still something told her to run. *Run, Mary, run!* Each tree was now a place to lurk or hide, each shrub a human form. There, crouched; there, standing. Bully was behind her, to the left, and to the right, and someone was ahead of her on the path. She could see him moving, coming towards her.

"Why don't you wait, Mary?" Bully's voice seemed to come from all directions. She turned to run across the green, but ran straight into him as he appeared out of the darkness.

"Oh Mary, this is great fun!" he grinned menacingly. "I'll tell you what I'll do: I'll count to ten and then come after you."

"Fuck off, Bully!"

"You don't like me, do you, Mary?"

"Look, Bully, whether I like you or not doesn't matter, but no, not particularly." It wasn't a good answer. It was what Bully expected, but not what he wanted to hear.

Bully was disappointed that she was wearing jeans. He had hoped she'd be wearing a short skirt, but he loved the shape of her hips and the curves of her thighs. He would prefer her to look slutty, like the prostitutes – like Katrina, with her overdone makeup and a skirt serving only to present her smooth legs and thighs, teasing the delight of their clients. Many times he relished standing in the shadows, watching them lean forward into punters' cars, with their mesh stockings, short skirts and chewing gum. It gave him perverse satisfaction imagining the services they provided, but often he didn't have to imagine. In the name of Stevie Pierce, he would cherry-pick them. It pained him that Mary was different, the bitch. He could smell the sweetness of her breath, hear her panting, and could almost feel the beating of her heart. Excitedly, he could sense her fear.

"But Mary, Mary, we've got something in common, you and me."

"There ain't nothing you and me have in common, Bully, and that's a fact."

"Oh, Mary, we should be friends."

"You're a liar and a cheat, Bully. That much I do know." Mary wished she hadn't said it. She shouldn't have said it. She felt Bully stiffen; she sensed his growing anger. She knew she should be appeasing and not provoking him.

Mary's rejection hurt. It hit Bully like a bullet in the heart. Dejected, rejected. *"I should have smothered him at birth!"* he heard his mother's cry. *"Smothered at birth!"* The words rang in his mind – tormenting words, disgusting words, hateful words.

"One, two, three," he began to count.

Mary, grabbing the sleeping Michelle out of the pushchair, turned and ran as fast as she could, trying to gain as much distance as possible, but then she stopped, realising she was running in the wrong direction. In her panic she had set off back across the grass in the direction of the cabin and the bandstand, and in her alarm she hadn't listened for where he was, whether he was where she had left him, or whether he had started after her. Perhaps he had overtaken her. She listened, gasping now for breath, her head turning this way and that, trying to decide. Then she thought she heard him – a crunch of leaves on the ground – but she couldn't tell from which direction the sound had come. Then she remembered that he was counting. She listened.

"Seven... eight... nine..."

She realised how futile it was trying to outrun him; with Michelle in her arms she couldn't do that. She had to hide first and then decide what to do. Reaching the cabin as fast as she could, she crawled through the undergrowth to hide at the back. But she soon realised that this was another mistake: they weren't going to be able to keep quiet enough. Michelle was now awake.

"I'm coming to get you!" Bully's voice penetrated the dark, echoing from all corners of the park.

"Mummy!" Michelle began, as Mary put her hand over her mouth.

"Shush!" Mary whispered. "Don't make a sound, pet."

Mary heard his heavy clumping footsteps and the rustling of leaves – first very close, then fading, distant steps. She heard the creaking of the cabin door opening and closing. And then the footsteps, louder now, rustling on the leaves and long grass. The silence was a deathly hush in which their breathing and heart beats seemed so much louder.

"Mummy!"

Mary's hand tightened over her daughter's mouth, desperately trying to keep her quiet. "Shush! It's all right, pet," she whispered. "We've got to stay very, very quiet."

But it was too late. Bully had crawled through after them and was now a monstrous leering form, reaching in to where they crouched on the ground. Mary tried to back away, but there was nowhere to go. The only way through the thick bushes and undergrowth was the way they had come. They were trapped in a hole where only a thin shred of moonlight penetrated the rambling scrub.

But for Bully too this hole was no good, as he realised to his great disappointment and frustration. He couldn't see enough. A grope in the dark was not enough, no matter how much he wanted to feel her body – to run his hands over her, to possess her. He wanted also to see her and particularly to see her fear. He wanted her to do as he wanted and he wanted to see her do it. This was no good. It wasn't as he had planned. It never was. The gap was just not big enough for him to squeeze through to reach her, crouched down as he was.

Reaching forwards, grabbing a leg, he tried to pull the child away from her mother. Mary held on to Michelle as tightly as she could. First she was afraid for Michelle, then she was terrified of her own powerlessness if he were to pull her away. Bully realised this too, which was why he now decided he would take the little girl if it took all his energy to do it. If he could pull the girl away, then Mary would be his. But it seemed impossible. Mary's grip was too firm. Her determination, the strength of a mother protecting her child, was too great.

Instinctively holding tight to Michelle with one hand, Mary scrabbled around with her other hand for something, anything to fend him off: a stick, a rock, an old bit of metal. Anything. Backing further into the crevice, trying desperately to get out of his reach, she felt a large stone or rock. She wasn't sure what it was.

It was hard, smooth, round, but what mattered was that it was hard. If she picked her moment, she might be able to use it to fend him off. There was little she could effectively do with it now. She could throw it at him, but with little force in such a small space. It was, she considered, better to wait for an opportunity or to use it if he came further in.

"Let go, you bitch. I won't hurt her, Mary."

Michelle began crying as Bully and Mary tussled over her. Holding the child's ankle tightly, Bully tried to punch Mary as hard as he could in the hope that she would release her grip, but still she held on. Realising that Mary couldn't defend herself while holding on to her child, Bully struck her again, his fist just reaching her body. He realised now that there was no turning back. He repeatedly punched and pulled with as much force as he could. He had to finish what he had started. A maniacal frenzy now possessed him, and with a mighty effort he pulled his big frame further in, stretching out his hand towards her. He was almost on top of her, scrabbling around almost blindly in the darkness. *Got her.* He'd done it. He could hardly move in the restricted space, but grabbing a handful of Mary's hair and twisting it round his fist, he pulled on it as hard as he could. Crying out, Mary reached up with one hand to grab his fist, loosening her grip on Michelle.

"I won't harm her," Bully hissed. "just let go, see, and I won't harm her, I promise."

"Please don't hurt her!" sobbing now, Mary released her grip as Bully pulled her child away from her, but still he held on to her hair, viciously tugging and twisting .

"You do as you're told and I won't harm her, understand?"

But he could not squeeze himself easily out of the gap. He wasn't stuck, but he couldn't keep his grip on both the child and Mary's hair. He would have to use one hand as support on the side of the cabin to help lever himself backwards out of the crevice. Slowly he pulled her out from behind the cabin with a firm grip on her hair, but he had no idea what to do next. He hadn't factored the child in at all, and the only planning he had done was to get Mary to the cabin.

"I won't harm her if you do as you're told," Bully repeated as he tried to decide what to do.

"I'll do what you want but don't harm her." Mary thought several times of making another fight for freedom; she hadn't given up. She felt around again to find the stone she had let fall in the tussle. She felt its round surface and rough edges. If she had a chance, she could use it. She held it tight behind her. Now she was thinking more clearly, and it was obvious he was crazy. She had to bide her time and make her escape when she could, and when she was also able to get Michelle out too. Meanwhile she would have to pacify him.

"Look, Bully, this is getting out of hand. Let's stop it now and just go home as if nothing had happened. I won't say anything, OK?" Mary sensed Bully's indecisiveness.

"It's too late for that now." Bully considered the option. "There's no way out now."

Mary could see that Bully was shaking. His voice was now stammering, mumbling, and she had difficulty understanding what he was saying. Slowly they edged out of the crevice, Bully still keeping a tight hold on Michelle and on Mary's hair, pulling it. The brambles around the opening scratched at his cheeks.

Bully pulled her into the dark cabin. She could see almost nothing until her eyes had adjusted. Bully pushed her to the back, away from the door, and she groped her way, bumping into objects and immovable bits of machinery. Suddenly the room was lit by Bully switching on a torch – a big industrial lamp with a beam so bright that it blinded her if she looked straight at it. She could see it move, but could see nothing but darkness behind. She could see neither Michelle nor Bully.

Bully placed the lamp on a dirty, heavy metal table that he tried to put in front of the door to bar the exit. It wouldn't budge, but even if she was to make a dash for the door, she wouldn't be able to get past his big frame. He now felt free to release the vice-like grip he had on Michelle, pushing her under the table.

"Mummy!" the child cried.

"It's alright, pet. Mummy's here!" Mary didn't want Michelle to be so frightened.

Bully tried desperately to collect his thoughts, to stay calm. He could feel the excitement growing. *"Don't damage the merchandise!"* But Mary wasn't merchandise, and he could damage her all he wanted. She wasn't owned by Stevie Pierce; she was his to do as he liked with, and the bitch wasn't going to tease him anymore. He took several deep breaths, trying to compose himself. He had to be firm; there was no turning back. But he wanted it to last; he didn't want to rush through panic. First he would talk. He would tell the little bitch a thing or two.

"Bully, what do you want?" Mary asked, breaking the silence first. "Why are you doing this? You won't get away with it."

"Shut your mouth, bitch!" Bully was furious that she had spoken first. "I'll tell you what I will get away with. You don't speak unless I tell you to." He glanced agitatedly around the room, his eyes darting this way and that, always back to Mary, planning what he would do and how. The cabin was cramped, with little room to move. It was full of piles of broken deckchairs, dusty old lawnmowers still caked in mud and dried grass from a bygone time, shovels, rakes and hoes. "Take your jumper off, bitch!" he ordered, his voice shaking with anticipation.

Chapter Seventeen: "Run Annie, Run!"

"Run Annie, run!" Rose was hopeless at finding places to hide. Her favourite spot was to tuck behind the old wooden cabin by the bandstand, but it was difficult to squeeze through because of the overgrown brambles and thistles. Annie wouldn't have minded that; she would have squeezed through anyway, but Rose couldn't do it, not this time. She was afraid of the creepy-crawlies and spiders. By the time she heard Charlie finish counting, she still hadn't decided. Annie had gone in the opposite direction, down to the brook, leaving Charlie at the bandstand, counting slowly with his back turned.

"It's alright Rose, I'm here." Suddenly Annie was there beside her, in a hazy twilight of perception as she lay in her hospital bed, time coalescing like shifting sand.

"Annie, is that you?"

"It's alright Rose, really," Annie's soft sweet voice reassured.

"I'm sorry, Annie! I'm so sorry!"

"It's alright Rose! It wasn't your fault."

"We should have waited for you, Annie! We should have waited! But we couldn't find you!"

"It's really alright, Rose. I should have come out and gone home with you."

"I missed you so much, Annie!"

"I missed you too, Rose!" It was an older Annie, an Annie grown up, as if she would have been. Yet the child was there too, as if they stood together, the older holding the hand of the child.

"Mary, Mary, quite contrary, how does your garden grow?" Bully's voice penetrated the dark.

Rose heard his voice first as Annie touched her arm and Bully Spence began menacingly to count, "One, two, three", and Mary ran fearfully with Michelle in her arms, crawling desperately behind the cabin.

"Mary? What is the matter? Why are you hiding?" Rose couldn't understand, but she sensed her daughter's fear. For Rose it was as if she was everywhere but nowhere. She could see Bully, but Bully couldn't see her as he ran up to the cabin and crawled in after Mary. He rushed past her like a film repeating itself, again and again. Several times she saw him rush past as though she wasn't there.

"Annie!" she called, but when she turned Annie was gone and Rose opened her eyes to the sound of a trolley rolling with a squeaking wheel somewhere in the hospital ward, and the muffled sounds of voices.

***

Paul was surprised on arriving at the hospital that Mary wasn't there. She hadn't been all day according to the nurses, which was odd because she visited every day at least for an hour, and she had said definitely that she would visit today after shopping.

"She's been very agitated all day and a bit delirious, I'm afraid," a nurse told him. "She has called for her daughter. Mary, isn't it? But most of what she says doesn't make much sense. She drifts in and out."

Paul was shocked by Rose's frailty: her sunken eyes, the bones of her cheek and jaw, a skull barely covered by a thin layer of skin, and the flesh of her cheeks drooping where her false teeth had been removed and placed in the glass on the bedside cabinet, as though they had removed her smile, taken her character and bottled it in water. It reminded Paul of his grandmother: her toothless grin and the large staring eyes, looking into a world she no longer recognised. She appeared to Paul as though she was shrivelling, ageing before his eyes as he watched, disappearing bit by bit, layer by layer as she lay in the metal bed with its rail guard to prevent her falling out, like a child in a cot. Like a child as she sounded now. Sitting in the bedside chair, Paul leaned forward to hear what she was saying: barely audible murmurings.

"Run, Annie, Run!" He heard her say. "Mary? Is that you? Why are you hiding?" the disjointed mutterings of a delirious woman.

He was touched, moved, but afraid. He felt awkward AND inadequate. He was anxious now for Mary to arrive so that they could deal with it together. *Come on, Mary, where are you?*

"It isn't Mary, Rose. It's me, Paul!" was all he could think of saying, trying desperately to restore sanity where he thought it was lost. "It's me, Paul!" he repeated awkwardly, hoping that repetition would penetrate where a simple utterance would fail. "Mary isn't here!"

"Paul?" Rose's dark eyes, stared into his like a frightened child's – a momentary flicker of recognition, a moment of fear like a frightened animal before a predator strikes. "Paul! Mary's here!"

"No, Ma, love. Mary isn't here. It's just me!"

"Come, Paul. You must come!"

"I'm here, Ma. I am here." It made little sense.

Rose, agitated, tried to lift her head. "Where is Mary?"

Where is Mary? He didn't know and it worried him. He had expected her to be at home, but she wasn't. He had expected to find her at the hospital, but she wasn't here either. Something was not right. And then there was the note left on the table in the kitchenette. It was his note, the one he had left for Bully Spence – the one he had left a week before, but not at the flat. He had left it at the Nag's Head for Bully. What was it doing at the flat and why was Mary not at home? Why was she not at the hospital? Where was Mary?

***

Annie kept so very quiet, so very still. She could hear the rustle of feet. First they were Charlie's, and she could see his polished black shoes with one of the laces undone. Charlie's shoes always shone. He polished them every day until they sparkled. He had the shiniest shoes in the school, but he rarely tied his laces. Somehow they would come undone, and he just couldn't be bothered to tie them again. So neat and ordered, was Charlie, and yet so uniquely strange, Annie thought.

"You'll trip over them, Charlie!" they would suggest.

"Haven't done!" would be his considered reply. Charlie always had a considered reply. He would often rub his chin, thinking, Annie thought, before making a simple observation. He would look far into the distance as if he could see a pearl of wisdom beyond. And now Annie could see it too, a wisdom beyond. He would watch a butterfly spread its wings, patiently watching. "That's a fritillary, is that!" Yet to Annie it was just a butterfly. "A brown fritillary!" he would add, on reflection.

"What makes it a fritillary, Charlie?" Annie would ask.

But Charlie would blush awkwardly with shyness, for Annie could do that to Charlie. "It just is!" he would reply.

She held her breath so as not to make the slightest sound, her heart pounding in her chest. She thought of springing out and surprising him, but then she heard Rose.

"Charlie, where is Annie?" Rose asked.

"I don't know. I can't find her."

Annie heard them walking casually away across the grass. It was the last she heard of them.

The silence of darkness descended so quickly. Yet it seemed she had waited just a few minutes before climbing out from her hiding place behind the culvert. She was going to run to catch them up. Her feet were wet, as were her clothes, from where she had crouched down in the wet mud by the brook. She had done what she often did: creeping from one hiding place to another, crawling under the hedges that lined the path. First she hid behind the cabin, squeezing through the thistles and brambles, oblivious to their sting, and then she had crawled through the railings into the shrubs behind. Finally, like a snake she had wriggled her way under the hedges down to the brook.

Charlie would be cross that she hadn't stayed in one place. Cheating, he called it. But Annie loved the thrill of not being found. She loved the tingling sensation of almost being discovered – almost but not, just a hair's breadth away. A thrilling 'almost'. So close, a foot almost touching her. So close that she could feel their breath on her cheek. She would hold her breath and stay very still and quiet.

But now there was silence, apart from the endless ripple of the brook, and it was getting late.

Crawling out, lithely slipping through the gap in the railings, Annie came to a sudden stop. As silently as she had hidden, he had appeared. Annie saw his big brown brogues first. A gasp; a beat of the heart. Annie was lost.

***

"Wait, Annie!" Rose called anxiously.

"It's alright, Mrs Harper," the nurse wiped a cloth over Rose's brow. "We're just going to adjust your pillow to stop you slipping down."

Rose opened her eyes but saw only a blurred image as she felt her body being lifted and pulled up.

"Where's Annie?" she asked. But the nurse didn't answer directly. Murmured voices, blurred and indistinct disembodied timeless voices, came and went.

"She's fading fast."

"It's alright, Mrs Harper. Your daughter is coming soon."

***

"Charlie is my darling, my darling, my darling.
Charlie is my darling, the young cavalier."

"What's a cavalier, miss?" one of the children asked the teacher.

"Does anyone know?" A chance never missed to teach.

Charlie put up his hand, eager to give his considered opinion. He knew the answer, he was sure. His dad had told him, because his name was Charlie. He eagerly pushed his arm up high, stretching to make it seen. *Me, miss! I know!*

"Yes, Charlie? Do you know?"

"Is it a knight, miss?"

"Yes, Charlie! It is a knight. A cavalier."

And Charlie beamed with pride.

***

"You're my knight, Charlie!" the voice said in Charlie's head, older now, with tears shed, his soul at the twilight of reality.

"Annie? Is that you, Annie?"

"Charlie is my darling, my darling, my darling.
Charlie is my darling, my young cavalier," Annie sang in Charlie's head.

- 163 -

It was a sweet, rhythmic sound. And Charlie sang too, and with beating drum he marched, up and down the path in the park, the light fading fast. He had picked up a large stick, a discarded piece of fencing to wield as a sword. A knight, Annie had said, must have a sword.

"You'll need a sword, Charlie. Pick up a sword!"

Charlie swung the stick over his head. "We'll smite the enemy!" he cried.

"As he cam' marchin' up the street, the pipes played loud and clear. And a' the folk cam' rinnin' out, to meet the cavalier." Annie loved the way *running* became *rinnin'*.

"Rin, Charlie, rin!" she would call. "You're a bonny prince, Charlie!"

"And you're a bonny lass, Annie!" Charlie mused. "And we were such wee 'bairnies', Annie! Such wee 'bairnies'!" They loved imitating a Scottish accent.

"Rum tum, tumpetty tum," the sound of the band they heard. "March, Charlie, my bonny prince!" Annie cried.

And in the twilight, dusky gloom, Charlie marched down the path leading to the brook and the bandstand. Annie followed behind. And Rose followed, joining behind, marching in step.

Onward, Charlie, onward! the beating drum impelled. And behind them followed a ghostly host of the lost and forgotten.

"You will be my lady, Annie, and Rose will be the queen!"

"And you will be our trusted knight!" Annie shouted. "Smite the enemy, Charlie. Knock him down!

Smite the enemy! Knock him down!" Rose and Annie chanted in unison. "Smite the enemy! Knock him down!"

"Smite the enemy! Knock him down!" repeated the ghostly host.

And Charlie saw the fair lady on the path, a shadow in the dusk, and he saw the enemy, the black knight looming. A shadow in the dark.

***

A fly buzzed aggressively around Bully's head, an intrusive irritation. He swatted it away, but back it came, persistently, and then another. He swatted at them again, but back they came, and then another and another, a host swirling round his head as a cloud. Flailing with his arms, spitting as they landed on his lips, he stepped back from the cabin door, shaking his head. But the more he flailed at them, the more they came.

It was a dull thud, the last Bully heard before he crumpled to the ground. He heard nothing else; he felt nothing else. It was the end – no time for pain, no time for reflection, just a dull thud as Charlie's stick found its mark, wielded by a knight, a cavalier.

"Strike him quick!" Annie had cried. "Strike him, Charlie, my bonny prince!"

"Strike him!" Rose had cried too. "Strike him, Charlie!"

"Strike him, Charlie! Strike him!" cried the host.

In the morning there would be the sweet smell of lavender and the song of a lark, another cavalier defending his patch. In the morning – not this morning, but another morning and the mornings after that, and when that lark had gone – another would take its place on the bough of the tree, a branch casting its lengthening shadow on the ground day by day, the unremitting passage of time. But this morning there were blue lights flashing, casting pale shadows in the dusky dawn, cutting, shrieking, telling all that something dreadful had happened, and instead of the dawn chorus of bird song, the chatter, clatter of walkie-talkies endlessly announcing "Foxtrot, Romeo, Alpha" while Mary with Michelle, wrapped in a blue blanket in the back of a police car, stared vacantly out of the window.

When they found her she was sitting cross-legged on the ground a few feet from the cabin where Bully Spence lay dead. Michelle was asleep in her arms as she rocked backwards and forwards, singing repeatedly and tunelessly as the tears flowed.

"Who shall have a fishy on a little dishy, who shall have a fishy when the boat comes in? Dance for your daddy, my little lassie, dance for your daddy when the boat comes in."

By her side was the 'stone' she had held so tight to use in her struggle. By her side they found the skull – a child's skull, the skull of a young girl.

"He just fell to the ground!" she had explained, as far as she could. "One moment he was attacking me, and then he fell."

She remembered only a vague silhouette, hovering like the moon behind a cloud. "Annie!" he had cried. "Don't worry, Annie, I'm here now!" And then Bully dropped, his eyes open wide like beacons in the dark.

A dull thud was all she heard, and then the silhouette had gone.

Annie had gone; Charlie had gone; Rose had gone. A wisp of wind now blew the leaves where their feet had once trod.

Epilogue

"I'm sorry I haven't visited for such a long time, Mum," Mary intoned softly, after she had sat reflecting in silence for a while on the park bench. "But we had to move away, get out of this place, and start afresh."

Mary reflected on the years that had passed since her mum's funeral. She had died the day she, Mary, had been attacked, and within a year after, they had moved away to start a new life.

"You did the right thing, love. It's not the same here now, not like it was in the old days."

"I know, Mum."

"They pulled the old factory down."

"Yes, Mum, they pulled the tower blocks down too. They've put such lovely little houses there now."

"Just as well, Mary, love. Them was horrible places to live."

"We moved to the seaside, Mum, me and Paul, and Michelle went to such a lovely school. Paul got a job – only a summer job at first, working in one of the arcades. He was a lovely dad to Michelle, but we never had any more children. He died when Michelle was ten. He had a brain tumour for years, they said. He was always getting headaches. By the time they found it, it was inoperable, Mum." Pausing for a moment, she held back a tear, a tear rarely shed, for the Lord had taken again, and she still didn't see why. "He had chemotherapy, but it didn't do much good. It just made him feel sick, so he decided enough was enough. You know he stopped swearing? He said he didn't want Michelle growing up around that."

"In the old days we was grown up proper, Mary love."

"Michelle's grown up now, and she's got a kiddie of her own! That makes me a grandma, Mum. How about that?"

Mary wondered if her mum was listening. She wondered if her mum was there at all. She had arranged the yellow daffodils in a small vase by the tree, her mum's favourites, while Michelle had gone off with Annie to get some ice creams.

"Nana, Nana", little Annie cried out as they returned. "The lady gave me a balloon!"

"What lady, sweetheart?"

"The lady over there!" little Annie replied. But when they looked the lady had gone.

Mary felt the wind on her cheek – a wisp, a flutter of leaves, a beat of the heart.

End

Printed in Great Britain
by Amazon

73924866R00098